Kisses

Jeannie Curran

Rev. date: 05/14/2015

To order additional copies of this book, contact:
Xlibris
800-056-3182
www.Xlibrispublishing.co.uk
Orders@Xlibrispublishing.co.uk
705899

Dedication

Kisses is dedicated to my mum and dad, Lily and John Glenn whom I love and miss every day. Without their love and commitment to each other and their five children I would not have had the tools to write my novel. I would not have had the memories of Culdaff and been able to bring them to life through my writing. Lots of love, kisses and hugs sent your way always.

Acknowledgments

To my family, my children, sorry for being there in body but not in mind. I'm not that sorry though because now I have 'Kisses' haha.

Thank you to Declan, my husband and bestie, editor and researcher when I hadn't a clue what to do next when I finished Kisses. You own all my 'kisses' always and forever babes, love you for as long as your . . . lol (wink wink)

Thank you to my one and only sister who encouraged me from day dot. Our mutual love of reading meant you could guide me in my writing and provided us with the best excuse to chat 'books' and all things girly. Love you forever sis and bestie.

Cheers to everyone who got excited for me and with me about 'Kisses' and finally to the people of Derry, the most amazing City, full of the most charismatic human beings in the most beautiful and historic town. Lots of 'Kisses' to you all. Please enjoy x

Chapter 1

Springtime, daffodils bunched along the roadside and in nearly every garden, signalling new beginnings, fresh starts. The children ran about with their wee milky white arms and legs bared after a long Irish winter in wool and fleece, their wee noses getting the first light scatter of freckles from the springtime sun. 'Springtime had to be the best time of the year,' Sally thought . . .

Easter was late this year, and in two weeks, she would take off for her mum and dad's mobile home in Culdaff, a beautiful part of the country not far from Malin Head, the most northern part of Ireland. The views and beaches were stunning even on a dull day, but if the Irish weather permitted and the sun came out, then that was a whole other experience for the eye.

Population was about 350, the last she had read a few years ago. It at least doubled in the summer months – everyone flocking to summer houses and mobile homes, some of which were like suites at the Waldorf Hotel. Sally's parents' mobile home was like that – three double bedrooms with an en-suite and a fitted state-of-the-art kitchen with a dishwasher, a washing machine, a full-length fridge freezer, and, of course, a wine fridge . . . of course. It had wrap-around decking and an eight-piece garden set with loungers to match. When the weather was nice, there was no more beautiful scenery and views that Sally could think of.

The site the mobile homes sat on overlooked a small beach, and hail, rain, or shine, you always saw the sea and at night the lighthouse. It had wash houses with five washer-dryer machines (for those who didn't have washing machines in their mobile homes) – everything one needed for a relaxing break away. Mc Gory's Hotel was a short drive away, which always had some kind of entertainment going on. It even got in the 'Hot Press Best of Ireland's Twenty Best Venues' and lots of other awards in Ireland. A ten-minute walk on the road led to another pub-come-guest house overlooking the beach. What more could one ask for?

Sally had two weeks off work and she couldn't wait to get away to one of the most peaceful and relaxing parts of the country she ever had the pleasure of coming across. Culdaff was like a different world. She knew as soon as she stepped foot out of the car and breathed in the country air she would feel the bliss . . .

Work was really stressing her out, and she really disliked her boss and she got the feeling that the feeling was mutual. Sally's title was 'supervisor' in a café in the town called 'Victoria's Café', but she more or less ran the café; she had hardly ever seen her boss, only when she was giving her friends a free lunch. Sally would agree Victoria was a 'hard-faced woman of the world' as Victoria would put it. (Sally added the 'hard-faced' bit in.) As Sally would put it, she was a 'hard-faced spoilt daddy's girl that never had to work for a thing in her life', and if that passed for an 'of the world' at the end of it, then so be it.

She had a chip on her shoulder, a rich daddy's little girl who expected everyone she employed to dance to her every tune. She would waltz into the café with her size-eight figure, all skin and bones, long waist-length dark brown hair flying around the counter and food, her nose in the air, and maybe order coffee for her friends and herself and leave without either a thanks or a payment.

She wasn't much older than Sally, which made it even harder for her to like her. Daddy's money had bought her the café, but she didn't care much for it; she just liked the feeling of empowerment of owning it.

Sally loved her job, colleagues, and the customers, most of whom she had grown to know personally. Lisa and Shelly were the other two full-time workers at the café, and they had a great laugh together. Lisa was thirty and Shelly forty-two. Shelly was a big girl with an even bigger personality. She had a heart of gold and always a smile on her face for everyone. Lisa was a lot quieter, but the different personalities among the three worked well, and they had a blast working together – always laughing and having the craic with each other or the customers. Sally worked hard and liked to be kept busy but never got the appreciation she deserved; she made it her business to give the other two girls the credit *they* deserved. She was taking this time out not only to relax but also to try and get her head around the fact that work was getting her down a little. She wanted to think about where life was taking her and what she really wanted from it. Her life was beginning to depress her just a little and that scared her a lot.

At twenty-six, Sally was five feet seven inches, with a great curvy body, long wavy blonde hair, Irish gypsy eyes (emerald green), and a great personality to match. Sally had her fair share of offers of dates. She didn't care much for any fellas she dated though. She went on dates sometimes, most of whom she dumped in a text the next day or didn't answer their calls after the first date. She even walked out of the cinema on one fella, telling him she was just popping to the loo, and off to home she went for a bath and a glass of wine, her Westlife album playing in the background. He never called her again, needless to say.

She left another fella in a restaurant. But then, he was a male chauvinist pig and deserved the humiliation. During dinner, he said, 'I am glad you don't feel intimidated by the fact I have a much superior job to yours. I mean, if you were to get married, you would be leaving your job anyway, so what's the use in wasting time with a high-powered job, right?'

'Excuse me,' Sally said to that, and off she went as if going to 'the loo', but she darted straight out the door and off to home. Her wine and Westlife album were both on standby . . .

She never met anyone who held her attention or her heart any more than a month.

Mal lasted eight months though. He was the one every boy was measured up to. No one ever came close, and Sally couldn't get him out of her head; sometimes she didn't even want to. He was her partner in science all of the fifth year, and on the last day of the school year, he asked her to go bowling with him. That was it; they spent the whole summer together, walking the back roads of the borders between Donegal and Derry and eating packed lunches on the dragon's teeth that separated the borders. Huge four-by-four-feet concrete blocks stopped cars from driving to and from Donegal without passing through the police checkpoint first. They would take one block each and sit with their legs criss-crossed over in front of them, eating their lunch of whatever was in the fridge that morning – from jam sandwiches to corn beef and HP sauce sandwiches, crisps and custard cream biscuits. Custard creams were always Mal's favourite. Every time she saw one, to this day, it still reminded her of Mal, of days spent walking without a care in the world, and of fresh air in bucket loads. She missed those carefree days, and at the thought of being in Culdaff for two weeks, with all its beautiful blue flag, sandy beaches, and mountains surrounding the field where the site was situated in, Sally's heart pounded in anticipation. It was everything she needed right now. Peace and quiet and some 'me time . . .'

Chapter 2

Sally's bbf was Nicole O'Shea. The girls were friends through everything – from nursery school to now. One of the incidents which their mums would tell them about fondly was when Nicole had been playing hairdressers in the nursery room. She had sat Sally down at the little pink plastic dressing table, got a pink comb and the arts-and-crafts scissors, and chopped and chopped at Sally's hair. She then squealed, crying because, thankfully, the scissors didn't cut the hair. They still got a laugh to this day at that story.

Their mums had lots of stories of both fights and a blossoming friendship. Another story was when the girls at age eight dressed up in their mums' clothes, put on a really full face of make-up, and went walking round and round the few streets next to theirs. They didn't want to go home because they thought they looked too grown-up and beautiful, so they walked to a café and sat there reading magazines and playing grown-ups. They didn't know their parents were going out of their minds with worry searching everywhere they could think of. They got their wings clipped for their disobedience at the time, but looking back now, they could all laugh . . .

The girls' mums had been friends from secondary school; both married two best friends and were inseparable ever since. When they fell pregnant within five months of each other and both had girls, Sally being the older of the two, it was beyond their best ever imaginations.

When Nicole was dumped by Johnny Brown in the third year of school, Sally and her mum, Elizabeth, went straight over to Nicole's with the largest tub of Dale Farm Raspberry Ripple Ice Cream, a bottle of ice cream soda, Maine fizzy lemonade to make ice cream drinks, and a six pack of flakes to sprinkle on top.

Elizabeth and Nicole's mum, Anna, sat at the kitchen island, drinking coffee and eating a flake each with two straws, ready to suck up the flaky chocolate bits that fell to the counter with every bite.

'You're never too old for chocolate and never too old to eat it the way you want to,' Anna had said. After twenty minutes of Nicole questioning herself and Sally reassuring her that it was 'Johnny Brown's loss', they went downstairs to make their drinks while their mums laughed and chatted about their old days; even knowing then that their mums would have been only about thirty-five, the days they talked about were old to them. Stories flowed, and the ice cream drinks sprinkled with flakes disappeared, and the four best friends in the world enjoyed their little haven of mother–daughter friendship. Bad Johnny Brown was never mentioned again . . .

Nicole, now an excellent colourist and stylist, (funnily enough) had her own hairdressers and beauticians in town and was doing great, loving her job and life. She had a boyfriend for the last three years – a lovely fella called Johnny White (what's the chances?); she had met him in a pub in Letterkenny one girls' night, but Sally forgave her because he was so cute, and they looked even cuter together. Being the same size as Nicole in three-inch wedges (Nicole in the wedges, not Johnny), it took him to about five feet ten inches; they had exactly the same colour of auburn hair and brandy-coloured eyes. They could have passed for brother and sister had it not been for the chemistry between them.

'Cute as two buttons together,' Nicole's mum, Anna, would say. She loved him 'nearly' as much as she loved Nicole.

Johnny had been eyeing Nicole up all night, and when he finally made his way over to their company, the music stopped, but Johnny still asked, 'Would you like to dance?' He was *that* nervous. The girls burst out laughing but then felt sorry for him when he went to leave. Sally stayed him with her hand on his arm and then very discreetly nipped to the ladies. When she returned, Nicole was on full flirt alert.

The girls were staying in the Ramada Hotel that night and taking the bus back to Derry the next day. Johnny saw this as an opportunity and insisted on driving them home the next afternoon. He was double-parked outside their hotel entrance from five minutes to twelve the next morning in his Honda Civic that was polished to within a millimetre of its metallic paint. He spent the day with Nicole in her mum and dad's house, had dinner, and then drove home. He drove up and down nearly every night, and within three months, he had a job in Derry, and they had a deposit down on a house to move in together. Nicole's dad was none too pleased about the arrangement, being kinda old-fashioned, but Johnny and Nicole were made for each other, and even Jim couldn't deny that. They were inseparable.

They sometimes reminded Sally of Mal and her; their summer together was the best of her life. The only thing that interrupted them for the full two months was the week in Portugal her mum and dad had booked. It was the first time they went away without Nicole and her mum and dad, and that was only because they had a family wedding in Chester, England, to go to and couldn't afford both.

Nicole and Sally would cast spells on the bride-to-be and her future husband. Having reached an age of sexual knowledge, they wished his penis to be twisted and bent so it would hurt her going in on their wedding night. They hated anyone who kept them apart. Jeez, the innocence of them, with a small twist of badness . . .

The summer otherwise was perfect. Sally had two very different best friends – Nicole for her girly chats and Mal for everything else. Mal was way too laddish to talk girly stuff, but she always felt she could talk to him about anything, and she knew the feeling was mutual. Life was good . . .

Mal announced on 7 February, eight months after they began their summer of carefree fun and cosy winter of movies, custard creams, and Wispa bars with Nicole and Brian Wade (a boy she dated just so she wasn't a gooseberry, she admitted years later), that his parents were splitting up, and his mum, originally from Madrid, was packing up and moving back to look after her elderly parents, who were eighty-three and needed her more than ever to help them with their farm and to assist them with life's comings and goings in their old age.

They stood surrounded with green grass, hills, and fresh Donegal air in the paddock of Lenamore stables, where they had walked to loads of times, but this time she knew he was hiding something from her. She didn't want to think he could, so she just babbled on about Nicole and her day at school. Nicole and Sally had gone back to school to do A levels, but Mal and Brian hadn't. Mal had gone to the training centre for school leavers to get himself a trade in the joinery. Brian had gone to work with his dad, learning the plumbing trade. Sally was in the middle of telling him about Nicole having a very grown-up debate in business studies class with their teacher Mrs M. Hamilton (they had to use the 'M' because there were three Mrs Hamiltons) when Mal grabbed her to his chest and squashed her head under his chin tightly, saying, 'Shh, Sal, please.' He patted her long curly blonde hair with his right hand and held her tight around her shoulders with his left. He was going to turn seventeen in less than a month and Sally had still two months to go to be seventeen, but it was a very real and grown-up moment they shared. Standing there in the field of horses in Mal's arms, Sally felt her heartbeats pound in her ears; she was both comforted and nervous. She did not know why Mal had been acting weird the whole twenty-minute walk there and then was so loving and grown-up and strong, holding her like . . . like he loved . . . 'Oh my God, was that it?' she thought. 'Is he going to tell me the three little words?' she wondered just as he let her loose but not free, holding both their hands together in the middle of their bodies; his features were taut. His beautiful nearly black eyes were framed with thick black lashes any girl would die for; his full lips opened and shut and opened and shut again as he just stared into Sally's emerald green eyes. Sally decided in that split second to put him out of his misery and in a breathy whisper blurted out, 'I love you too, Mal . . .'

Chapter 3

Sally and Nicole decided a girly night was long overdue, as were Sally's roots. Most of the time Sally went to the salon, but when she couldn't fit in hair appointments with work hours, she would go to Nicole's three-bedroom semi she owned with Johnny to get her naturally blonde hair touched up with a few highlights. Nicole said if she let Sally run round with those roots any longer, being Nicole's best friend, it would give her a bad rep as a bestie and a colourist. So poor Johnny was sent packing, and Nicole and Sally ordered Chinese food, bought two bottles of wine each (the food would soak up most of the wine), and got started on Sally's highlights. The food arrived just as Sally went upstairs to wash her hair, so she washed it twice as quick. Nicole lit candles on the beautiful six-seater's smoked glass top table, laid place mats, and moved to one side her vase of forget-me-nots and fuchsias, meaning forget me not and humble love. Nicole loved flowers and always bought herself a bunch of peonies every weekend from Sainsbury's while she would be there doing her shopping, but after reading *The Language of Flowers* by Vanessa Diffenbaugh a year and half ago, she found out they meant 'anger' and never looked at them again. She had a beautiful, albeit small, garden with two red rose bushes on each side of her front door, meaning 'love'.

There were two orange rose bushes on each side of the gate that led a straight pathway to the front door, meaning 'fascination', and two purple rose bushes at each end of the front of the house, meaning 'enchantment'.

Under no circumstances could anyone buy her yellow roses, as yellow roses meant 'infidelity'.

Nicole had 'wisteria' in pots on her front steps, meaning 'welcome', and flower pots placed in order of colour, full of tulips meaning 'declaration of love', next to each rose bush, like the red roses with pink tulips, the orange roses with purple tulips, and the purple roses with yellow tulips.

It was a fairy-tale garden and listening to Nicole talk you through it all, with their meanings and why she put one colour and flower type with the other, was infectious.

They sat together yumming and humming their appreciation for the chicken chow mein with satay sauce. The wine went down as good as the Chinese, and the girls chatted about their life and dreams, like they always did. They put on the *Sex and the City 2* DVD; they could act the bloody film out because they had watched it so often, but they knew full well they wouldn't get to watch it completely as they would chat way too much throughout it. The night was just what the girls needed; life was so busy that when they finally got together and relaxed, it was amazing, and it just reminded the girls of how much they loved each other, just like sisters.

Johnny arrived home from gym and an extra-long visit to his mum and dad's house in Letterkenny (a forty-minute drive away) and found the girls sitting on the cream corner sofa, bare feet tucked up under themselves, laughing and giggling with wine swooshing about in mid-air, but amazingly not a drop spilt.

'Oh,' Sally said, 'it's home time.'

But Nicole wouldn't hear of it. It was only eleven fifteen on a Saturday night. 'There is a spare room with a plaque saying "Sally's room" on the door,' Nicole sang.

'Seriously?' Sally asked, giggling. Then lifting her eyebrows, she slurred, 'Awwwww.'

'Naw,' said Nicole, giggling too, 'but I am sending Johnny to get you one made in the morning. Your reaction was *way* too cute.'

Laughing together, Johnny and all, they went to the kitchen where Johnny had got himself a chicken box and brought the girls a bag of chips for chip butties. The girls sat at the table again, and Johnny set everything out: bread and butter, tomato ketchup, and side plates. He opened the bag of chips, and the smell of vinegar and salt wafted right up their noses and made their mouths water.

'How are your mum and dad, babes?' Nicole inquired.

Johnny filled up their wine glasses and settled down to eat too.

'Aye, they're grand sure nothing ever changes down in that neck of the woods,' he replied.

'Wee fatsos tonight,' mumbled Sally in between her chewing of chips and wiping of the ketchup sauce and melted butter that dripped to her chin. More giggles followed, and that was the last they remembered before they hit the pillows sleeping or K.O.-ed, as Johnny would say the next morning.

BLT toasties, made with maple bacon (always maple bacon), and sparkling water the next morn was just what the doctor ordered.

'Johnny really is a saint,' Sally said sincerely to Nicole.

'I know,' mumbled Nicole, picking at a stray tomato. 'I think I'll keep him.'

Johnny just laughed and asked how their heads were and if they needed headache tablets. Sally left Nicole and Johnny, and before she was out past the orange rose bushes at the entrance gate, they were back in bed 'huggling' as they called it, a mixture of hugging and cuddling . . . Yes, yes, that's just how cute they are.

Sally loved Nicole and Johnny to bits but sometimes felt like a gooseberry. It was probably the same way Nicole felt when Sally had Mal and she dated Brian Wade, just so she wouldn't feel like one. Sally thought of the day she stood in the field at Lenamore stables, the day her love life fell apart and was never the same since. At sixteen, Sally classed Mal as her bbff (bestest boyfriend forever) and the love of her short life, which even at sixteen she knew was hard to find. Nicole was dating Brian but didn't have what Sally and Mal had between them. Lots of girls were dating boys, but no one was dating their best friend by one. His eyes, when she told him she loved him, welled up, and he dropped to his knees, saying, 'I am going to miss you so much, Sal.'

'What? What did you just say?'

She dropped to her own knees and pulled his beautiful head out of his hands with all her strength. 'You're dumping me?' she managed to say, trying hard to see into his eyes, and when he just looked at the flattened blades of grass under him, shaking his head, she got up and ran – ran until she stumbled because she couldn't see with the tears stinging her eyes and the weight of her heart in her tummy. 'How could he? How could he?'

She was spitting when she got home and eventually told half the story of why she was so distressed. Elizabeth put her arms around her whole body, shushing her, telling her everything would be OK. John folded his newspaper, ruffled her hair, and phoned Anna and Nicole. Nicole's dad, Jim, drove the girls over, stopping on the way for Dale Farm Raspberry Ripple Ice Cream, ice cream soda, Maine fizzy drinks, and a six pack of flakes.

The dads sat in the living room, watching boxing. Elizabeth and Anna were both at the dining table in the kitchen with coffee, flakes, and straws, and the girls lay on Sally's daybed in her room. Sally's face was buried in her pillow that was now stained with both snot and mascara.

'No amount of ice cream drinks is going to fix this, Nicole,' sniffed Sally. 'You don't know what it's like. I thought we would be together forever.'

She stuffed her head under the pillow and curled up in a ball. Nicole had never felt so helpless, never felt so shut out of Sally's life before that very moment. Not knowing what to do or say, she left Sally in her room alone. Sally vaguely heard the bedroom door open and close; then minutes, maybe hours later, she heard it open and close again. She felt and then smelt her mum lie on the bed beside her; Elizabeth's Channel No. 5 perfume filled the air between them. She patted Sally's long blonde hair, just like Mal had less than an hour ago. After a long silence, with only sobs and sniffles interrupting it, Elizabeth said, 'Do you want to talk to him, darling?'

'No, Mum, I never want to see him again. I hate him' was Sally's reply, and then she broke into another heartbreaking sob.

'I know, darling, but he's downstairs and wants to explain. I will send him away if that's what you want. It's your choice, darling. You don't have to do anything you don't want to,' said Elizabeth in her most relaxing and calming voice.

After a minute, Sally thawed; the thought of Mal downstairs made her want to go down and throw her arms around him, and hopefully, he would wrap his arms around her and tell her it was all a big mistake, that she had misunderstood the whole thing. Then all of a sudden, her feelings changed; she didn't know if she wanted to slap him or kiss him. He said he was going to miss her. 'Maybe he is only going away for a week or something,' she thought with a glint of hope. 'Maybe he is going on a trip for work stuff.' She felt flushed with anticipation and her spirits picked up a little.

'Can you ask him to give me an hour and then call back, Mammy, please?'

'Of course, I will, darling.'

Getting up together off the daybed, Elizabeth went to the door and Sally to her en-suite . . .

Chapter 4

When Sally got home from Nicole and Johnny's house, she showered and changed, feeling a little bit better after it; her head was still fuzzy and her mouth felt like a fur boot, but nothing her sparkling water and head-ease tablets couldn't see to, although she wished they would speed up a little. She put on her 'Sunday best', as Elizabeth would call 'your good attire', and went for a walk up the quay; it was a beautiful day, sunny and fresh, with a bite in the air that made you wear both a scarf and sunglasses. It was her favourite kind of weather, and as her head was still a bit fuzzy from the night before, a walk up the quay would definitely assist the water and pills in bringing her round before dinner at her mum and dad's. It was a Sunday ritual. Weekdays were busy for everyone, but Sundays were Mum, Dad, and Sally's day. Elizabeth had been saying this for as long as Sally could remember. The only people allowed to gate-crash were Anna, Jim, and Nicole, but even that was only an odd occasion.

The promenade was packed with people out on Rollerblades and bikes and mums and dads pushing prams and trying not to clip other pedestrians with the wheels. There were even two girls about Sally's age on retro-style roller boots; they looked brand new, with bright white leather boots, white wheels, white laces, and even the stoppers were bright white. 'Must be their first day out on them,' she thought. They looked so cool, and Sally decided straight away she would go online that night and search for a pair for her and Nicole. It would be more fun than the gym.

The smell from the big beautiful hanging baskets that lined the quay scented the crisp air and seemed to freeze in her brain. As she walked up past the marina, she watched the boats sit as still as the water allowed, their reflection clear as crystal on the mirror of The River Foyle. With each step she took she got more of a spring in it, and before she knew it, she was up at the Peace Bridge. A work of art in the form of a foot bridge, it was built to join the Derry side to the Waterside; its shape and position across the water and what it stood for in a city that had had its fair share of troubles made it all the more beautiful. She settled on a bench overlooking the iver and the bridge; the water sat still today for a change, as it's usually one of the fastest running rivers in Europe. It sat high with the sun shining on it, making it look like a glossy, exotic holiday picture fit to represent a destination in Bora Bora or somewhere alluring. The sun also shone on the glass dividers of the bridge and on everyone's faces passing, giving everyone a feel-good look in their eyes. Daffodils gathered in huge bunches, planted every four feet in three-by-three feet planters all along the walkway. The railings held huge big flower boxes that housed a ray of flowers that were so colourful it was like an explosion in a paint shop. The city was at its most beautiful, and in that very moment, Sally felt very proud of it and its people.

She took a deep breath in and exhaled, and as she rose to her feet to start back down the quay she spotted her mum and dad nearing the end of The Peace Bridge and stopping at a very traditional-looking ice cream vendor. 'With his stripy apron and straw hat, he looks like something from the forties or fifties,' she thought. Sally called out, 'Mum, Dad.'

John shook the man's hand, saying goodbye, and Elizabeth waved, standing on her tiptoes as she linked arms with her husband. They made a striking couple. Elizabeth once had light blonde hair much like Sally, but now it was more a sandy blonde, her eyes still as blue as the sky that played a backdrop to her. In a brown faux fur thigh-length coat and black jeggings, her figure was what some eighteen-year-old girls would die for. Her time spent at the gym was paying off – every weekday without fail. Her hair was blowing in waves atop her shoulders; it was said on a few occasions that she was like a blonde Liz Hurley with her high cheekbones and a great figure to rival. She was an equal next to John, a handsome man of forty-seven with silver hair but a young sharp face, emerald eyes just like Sally's, broad shoulders, and long legs that took him to six feet exactly. As they came together, they all hugged and walked back down the quay towards their cars, each of John's arms taken by the most precious people in the world to him.

They chatted about how beautiful the day and their city were. Elizabeth was telling Sally about their plans for Easter. They were going down to Rosses point in Sligo for a three-night, four-day break with Anna and Jim. Their hotel overlooked the point and had the most stunning views, she said. Elizabeth said she wished Sally would come with them instead of going to Culdaff on her own, but she knew when Sally made her mind up, it wasn't to be changed again, but the offer stood. When they got back home, they shared memories of their earlier days in a mobile home in Culdaff. The mobile was not as luxurious in those days, and they had to walk to collect canisters of water and to use the outhouse toilets. They spoke of walking over the mountains for hours, passing sheep that just chewed their grass, lazily looking up with no emotion in their eyes whatsoever. They would walk to the edge of the mountain and look into 'dead man's cave', named so because the story was that if you fell in, you didn't get out alive because of its shape. There was nothing to climb on, and the rocks all curved up and in, swallowing the cave and everything in it. They laughed at the stories that were told about 'Flying Louie', a weird middle-aged man that rode a bicycle everywhere. It was said he had thrown his wife off the mountain and into dead man's cave, just to see if she could fly (hence his nickname), and that he was always on the lookout for a new wife and wanted kids too. Every child was scared of Flying Louie, so when their mum said, 'Don't leave the site,' they didn't . . .

The tales stretched on over dinner of roast leg of lamb, root veg, cream potatoes, and mint sauce, an Easter dinner one week early, and it was delicious as all Elizabeth's dinners were. When Elizabeth suggested Sally should go up to her old room and find the old photo albums in her wardrobe, Sally jumped up like an excited child, ran upstairs, and found her room just as she had left it four years ago, everything in its place. She opened the wardrobe and found at least twenty albums, all with the years and occasions handwritten on them; the albums were stacked from the floor up to one side of the wardrobe, all different sizes but stacked and made up from largest to smallest, earliest to latest in three rows. She took after her mum in many more ways than her looks. It would take her hours to get through all these, and then a thought occurred to her. She would take them with her to Culdaff; it would be the perfect place as she needed to look at every photo one by one. It must have taken her mum ages to do this. She spied 'Culdaff 1995'; Sally would have been seven. She pulled it gently out of its place and left a sheet of A4 file paper hanging slightly out of its spot instead so that she would know exactly where to return it to. When she got downstairs to the kitchen, her mum had made coffee and put some pizza biscuits on a plate. (This was what she used to call shortbread petticoats when she was young because of their triangle shape, and it just stuck with them – even Anna, Jim, and Nicole calling them the same without a second thought giving.) Sally admired Elizabeth's handiwork on the albums, and Elizabeth admitted it had taken awhile to do but was worth every minute spent. Sally asked if she could take the albums with her to the mobile, and knowing Sally was as particular with her stuff as she, Elizabeth agreed. They looked through the album, laughing at hairstyles and outfits, pointing out silly jewellery and Elizabeth's dark lip liner. The dark lip liner made Elizabeth look like Sally, who at the age of six had painted her lips with a kohl eye pencil. There were photos of Sally and Nicole in a field full of sheep, Nicole hanging out of an abandoned tractor and Sally in the driver's seat.

'Always in control,' said Elizabeth in a proud voice. 'The one and only time I've seen you lose control was over Mal.' Silence stayed in the room, and Sally kept her head in the album for a few beats to catch her breath; they had never spoken of Mal after he left for Spain.

He had turned up exactly an hour after he was asked to by Elizabeth. She had told him to give Sally that hour to get her head straight, and when he came back, he should be the most honest he ever was in his life. There was a slight warning in her soft tone, but she could see the distress on his face and felt for him in a way she hadn't expected. She thought she should have demanded John to go 'have a word', hold him by the scruff of the neck, fist eye level, and give him a warning about breaking their little girl's heart.

That awful day flashed in front of Sally's eyes now, like it had done for the last ten years. Sally had walked the stairs down to the entrance hall. Mal sat at the phone table, his shoulders stooped over and hands joined in front of him as if in prayer. She had showered and dried her hair, leaving her soft curls resting on her shoulders. She had put on a pretty floral top and jeans and reapplied mascara; she had painted her toenails a bright pink, although the colour of neither it nor the top matched her mood. She looked nice and tried to think positive thoughts but felt like a deflating Lilo, abandoned and sinking deeper and deeper into the sea.

When she reached the second-last stair, he leapt to his feet, instantly reaching for her hands with his two, and just as she always did, she let him hold them, his silent agony betrayed on his beautiful face. He then dropped one of her hands; keeping the other in both his hands, he led the way to the kitchen and they stood at the island, just looking at each other with heavy hearts. He rubbed her soft knuckles with his rough thumb; when he bent slightly with questioning eyes and took her mouth in a very tender loving kiss, she let him, her heart jumping out of her skin. She didn't know if it was her heart or his at one stage and decided in a corny, lost-in-the-moment kind of way that their hearts were beating as one . . .

Mal went on to explain that his dad had left his mum and was moving to America to take up with a girl less than half his age. His mum was broken-hearted; Mal said he'd never seen her so sad and shattered. Mal's mum told him she didn't have anything to keep her there in Derry now, only Mal. She was going to move back to her parents' farm in Madrid because her mum and dad had been in desperate need of her help the last few years and now was as good a time and excuse as any to move away from the memories she would be surrounded with if she stayed. She needed Mal to come too; she said that she couldn't live without him and that he was everything to her. Sally thought his mum was being very selfish, making him leave and guilt-tripping him into it. She thought that she couldn't live without him, and he was everything to her too, but she didn't say that; she could have been selfish, but she knew he was going through enough. He was to leave the following week; they agreed to meet up every day until he left, but after he left her home that evening, she never saw him again. He was busy packing and doing stuff for his mum in preparation for the move, which took place three days earlier than planned, and she was too busy soaking her pillows with salty tears.

He had posted her a letter just before he left, and she got it on the day he was supposed to leave.

> *My beautiful Sal*
> *This is the hardest thing I have ever had to do – leave you and write this. I can't imagine my life without you, but it has to be this way for a short while, at least, I hope. I will write to you every weekend, and I hope and pray you write back to me.*
> *I promise you I will see you again soon.*
> *Mal x*

That was the only letter she had ever received from him, telling her he wasn't as sincere as his words sounded in his letter, but even knowing this, it didn't make the hurt of losing him go away. She pined for him all day every day for a long time. She ached for his friendship, their laughter together, and his strong arms around her body, his hand stroking her cheek. The thought of him moving on without her was excruciatingly painful at times, but never ever did she feel hatred towards him – just longing for him and still love, always love.

'Yeah, Mum, I remember,' she said now with a sigh. 'How could I forget?' She rolled her eyes.

John was 'the quiet man'; he always seemed very much at ease with himself in all surroundings. He lived for his wife and little girl, as she would always be. When he saw Sally's reaction still after ten years, he couldn't help but react himself. As always being straight to the point, he spoke, 'He's been in contact, pet.' (It was a name he'd had for Sally all her life.) 'He rang my work, wanting to speak to me. I wasn't available, and he left a number for me to ring him back. It's a Spanish mobile number, so I assume he's still in Madrid.'

Sally's mouth fell open; her head was spinning, her heart fluttering like a wee bird trying to keep airborne. She felt excited most of all, her heart racing on before her head could catch up. She had to control her heart though. Chances were he wanted something from her dad; after all it was him he had contacted.

'Did you speak to him?' she asked in a low voice.

'Not yet, pet. We wanted to mention it to you first.' John nodded towards his wife, who stood deathly still, waiting on her daughter's reaction to the news that could possible change her life. 'Would you like me to?' Her dad had so much love and respect in his answer that she burst out into tears, but they weren't sad tears; they nearly felt like relief for some reason.

'Aw . . . aye, sure, just ring him, Dad . . . please.'

Sally got up, hugged her mum and dad very tightly, and went home to her apartment a little earlier than she would have normally, having a mixture of feelings. Elizabeth was a little worried and wanted to go with her, but she reassured her mum the best she could and off she went alone. Her first instinct was to ring Nicole, but she wouldn't. It was latish, and Sally felt exhausted; she poured herself a glass of white wine, put on her Westlife album (reserved for pining for Mal), and melted into her big cuddle chair, allowing herself to inch a little closer to her dream of cuddling on her cuddle chair with Mal . . .

Ten songs later and a bottle of wine polished off, Sally was ready for bed to face the world in the morning; she needed at least eight hours . . .

Work came and went in a bit of a blur. At the end of her shift, just as Sally was getting into her beloved red beetle, a twenty-first birthday prezzie from her mum and dad, she heard a text come through.

> *I rang the no. but no ans didn't leave msg will try again tomorrow. Keep u posted pet.*

Her heart might as well be up and down the quay on those roller boots she was yet to look for, for her and Nicole, she thought. Just the thought of her dad having his number made her weak. She drove home, got the laptop out, and searched eBay for the roller boots; every two seconds, Mal Quinn invaded her mind and heart, so it took her ten times as long. She bought two pairs of size 5, paid for next day delivery, and texted Nicole.

> *Hope u got me that plaque for my bedroom door at urs cuz i got a surprise for u xxxx*

A text came back in seconds. Sally knew Nicole was like a child on Christmas morn when she heard the word 'surprise'.

> *Omg am soooo excited plzzzz say you're outside my front door rite now with it plzzzzz xxxx*

Sally laughed, a real belly rumble laugh, throwing her head back, as she thought how cruel she was being, saying Nicole would have to wait twenty-four hours. Hopefully, the post wouldn't let her down. Before she got a chance to text back, another text beeped through.

> *Am looking out my window and ur not at my front door? Xxxx*

Her nose wrinkled up as she thought, 'Oh shit', and texted back.

Lol u will have to wait till the post permits xxxx

Can't believe you're making me wait Sally May Mc Quire you can wait for your name plaque too. I might even get fbff under your name x

'Only one x,' Sally thought. They always did four. 'Jeez, she's taken this waiting thing bad, even worse than I knew she would.'

What does fbff mean? and I paid over the odds for next day delivery so hopefully they will be here for us this time tomoro xxxx (4x's) « c?

k k k fbff means former best friend forever but of course I don't mean it xxxx can't wait for tomoro now love u xxxx Lol but u know I hate waiting . . .

love u too drama-rama xxxx text u asa xxxx

Thankfully, the roller boots did come the next day, and Sally was able to text Nicole with the good news.

Meet me at Sainsbury's car park up the quay at 7 tonight got your prezzie. Dress for a walk/workout lo xxxx.

Walk/workout? xxxx buzzing lol xxxx

Chapter 5

At seven o'clock, Sally was already suited and booted, elbow and knee pads in place, looking like a wee foal taking its first steps on shaky legs. Nicole jumped out of her car, squealing and jumping up and down with excitement.

'Oh my God, how and where the hell did you find these?' Nicole sang in high-pitched notes. 'I love them, but it's been ages since I was on roller boots.'

'Me too, I can barely stand,' laughed Sally.

Johnny was to leave her off and go to the gym, but when he saw the surprise, he just had to 'see this'; he was laughing his head off at the thought of the two girls on these roller boots, and if Sally's attempt was anything to go by, this was going to be good craic. When Nicole stood up, one leg shot out from under her and then another. She fell flat on her backside; that wiped the smile off Johnny's face, and he came running to help her to sit up on the bench she had just stood from. She sat on one cheek, sore but laughing and rubbing at her lifted cheek; they all laughed together, but Johnny wasn't convinced it was a good idea. Still he left them to it anyway, bidding goodbye because he couldn't stand watching it any more.

The girls 'found their feet'; they were 'on a roll' and laughed and swished past men, women, children, and pets out walking and cycling (pets were always walking). They had a ball and a workout at the same time.

'This was the most fun I've ever had working out in my life. Thank you so much, Sally,' Nicole said as they got back to Sally's car forty-five minutes later. She threw her arms around Sally's neck, which nearly took them both to the ground, ending in another bout of laughter. As they sat on the bench to remove their boots, Sally sighed deeply, enough to make Nicole's head turn to her, but before she could ask what's up, Sally had it out.

'Mal's been in contact with my dad.'

'Ohh Jaysus Mary, Joseph, and the wee donkey.'

Sally could do nothing but laugh a full rumbling sore belly laugh at Nicole's drama-rama reply; when she stopped and looked at Nicole, her face was still full of shock.

'Tell me everything right now, Sally May.'

Sally laughed again. 'Why? Am I in trouble?' When Nicole said 'Sally May', she knew she was in trouble, and when she said 'Sally May Mc Quire', she was in big trouble. Nicole was a true drama queen! Sally told her everything, which took her all of two minutes.

Nicole listened thoughtfully; then she let out a little squeal and clasped her hands in front of her heart and, in a dreamy state, said, 'Aww, your first and only love. This is soooo romantic.'

'What? What's so romantic? He rang my dad,' Sally replied, used to Nicole's overactive imagination, but even she couldn't predict what nonsense was about to follow.

'What if he's thought about nothing but you the last ten years? He's a hollow man. He's realised it's because he doesn't have you by his side every waking moment. He's come back to get you, and he's going to ask your dad for your hand in marriage.' Nicole's arms flew out as if she was on stage and about to get 'a standing ovation' for her dramatics.

'Whaaatt?' Sally shook her head. 'If he thought of nothing but me, he could have put pen to paper. Nicole, you are on fire tonight. That's the most shit I've ever heard from you in all the time we have known each other, and I've heard some shi—'

Nicole cut her off. 'I feel it, Sally.' She took Sally's hands in hers. 'Let's go to the garden centre.'

'What? Why?' Sally's vocals were stuck on 'W' throughout this conversation.

'Because I am going to plant a flower for you – not for you exactly, but for you and Mal. I am sooo excited.' Nicole jumped up as if the bench had burnt her ass. Sally could do nothing but laugh at Nicole's infectious enthusiasm, but her head wouldn't let her heart get carried away, although every once in a while, her heart skipped on and took over her head . . . It was nice.

After stopping off for Nicole's purse and *The Language of Flowers* book, they drove to the garden centre, slightly concerned about their sweaty bodies and clothes but more excited about this magical flower they were about to buy. Sally produced a bottle of Dove from the glove box in her car, and they had a quick spray to freshen up, if only a little.

They looked about, dipping to smell and feel the petals gently. Nicole had her book in front of her, looking at pictures and references; she pointed out camellia (my destiny is in your hands) but said that was too one-sided. When Sally looked over Nicole's shoulder, her eyes flicking over names and meanings of flowers beginning with Q, she stretched around Nicole and tapped at 'Queen Anne's lace' (Ammi majus), meaning 'fantasy'.

'You should surround yourself with these,' she said fondly, laughter in her voice.

'Ha ha,' said Nicole, a false disgusted look on her face. 'Can you take this a bit more seriously please, Sally May?'

'Oh, Sally May is back. I better get into some serious flower-picking mode,' thought Sally with a wee smile on her face. Looking at Nicole so determined made Sally love her more, if possible.

'Got it,' Nicole squealed after about half an hour of Sally following her about, stopping every two steps and checking the book. 'You don't have a garden, right?'

'Right,' agreed Sally, thinking she had never even thought about that herself.

'So it needs to be a house plant, right!' It wasn't a question, so Sally didn't answer. Nicole continued, 'A cactus! It requires little watering, so you won't kill it by not remembering it's there, although hopefully you won't forget, because it's going to work wonders. Look.' She pointed at the flower and meaning. 'Cactus means ardent love, intense feelings, and passionate and fervent love. It's perfect, but I can plant something myself in my garden for you two lovebirds. I pick honeysuckle – 'devotion', mine to you both and yours to each other.'

Sally's heart swelled; her best friend was a fruit cake, but she loved her friend more than she had ever thought possible in that very minute.

Sally arrived home after dropping Nicole off first. A shower was all she could think of until she was home alone with her magical flower.

She had always thought of a cactus as a tree, not a flower, but this little flower stood about a foot in height, half foot wide, with pink flowers on the cactus spines and in a pale pink pot which Nicole said would match the wallpaper on Sally's hearth wall and her hall.

'And because it's pink, it will give the girl the upper hand.' Nicole nodded and added a girly wink.

'Does it say that in your little book?' Sally had asked.

'Yes,' said Nicole, tapping her head. 'In my little Nicole O'Shea's book, "wise friend should listen to bff if she wants to lure first love back into life."'

'Jeez, you're not wise, woman,' Sally said, putting an arm around Nicole's shoulder, walking out of the garden centre.

'No,' said Nicole, 'you're the wise one . . . In the book, you're the wise friend, and I am the author of . . .'

'I know,' said Sally, laughing and pulling her closer, 'you dork!'

Sally wondered where to put the flower now and shifted it from a few different surfaces until she decided on her little hall table, between her front door and bedroom door. There was a photo of her and Nicole already on the table, but she thought they fit together, saying Nicole had picked it for her – well, for Mal and her.

Wednesday night was girlie night – girls being Nicole and Anna, Sally and Elizabeth; they took turns going to each other's house. They only lived about a twenty-minute round taxi drive from each other. It was a 'school night' as they say, so one bottle of wine each was all that was allowed. Nibbles of nuts, crisps, cheese and crackers, and mother–daughter bff laughter were mandatory. It was Sally's turn tonight; she was busy setting out the crackers and slicing the applewood smoked and Mexican chili cheese with a potato peeler to get it nice and thin, just how she and her mum liked it. Nicole and Anna liked theirs thicker and cut it themselves as and when they wanted it. Elizabeth had a key to Sally's apartment, so when Sally heard a small rattle at the door and the key opening it, she knew their night of fun was just about to begin. The girls settled around the four-seater oak table with high-backed cream leather chairs, each chatting about their week and the week to come; it was the Easter weekend, and everyone had plans.

Then Nicole piped up, saying, 'Show Mum and Elizabeth your flower, Sally.' And, of course, the topic of conversation led to Mal and his mystery phone call. Everyone already knew about it, but it was the first time they were all in the same room talking about it. Sally showed them her flower, and Nicole narrated the meaning. Sally felt a little foolish and slightly embarrassed. Her mum and Anna both thought it was a lovely idea, but her mum did add her famous philosophy.

'If it's meant for you, it won't pass you . . .'

Chapter 6

One o'clock on Thursday, Sally would finish work for two weeks, and it couldn't come quick enough. She had every kind of customer today, from the complainers to the loveliest and, of course, her admirer. Michael was about twenty-eight; he came in most mornings for a coffee, always chatting and full of life. He had a cheeky grin that was quite cute, dark hair that he kept shaved tight and green eyes - much like her own.

'Looking hot as always, Sally,' he called this morning, coming through the glass doors.

Sally just smiled and called back, 'Charmer'; she took it in her stride, knowing full well he *was* a charmer and probably spoke to half the girls in Derry that way.

'And what about me?' Shelly called from behind the hatch in the kitchen.

'No one comes closer to Sally than you do, Shell,' he said, winking at Sally.

Laughing and shaking her head, she made his double-shot latte without having to be asked and passed it to him across the counter.

'Fancy going for a drink this weekend, Sally?' His voice was low and sounded genuine; it had lost the cockiness she was used to hearing in it.

He took her by surprise, so she stuttered a little before answering, 'Sorry, Michael, I am heading away for a week or so.' Sally nearly felt bad for turning him down and very nearly changed her mind just so she wouldn't hurt his feelings.

'No probs, babes, maybe another time.' He was back to his cocky self just in time for Sally to come to her senses. Walking out the door, he turned and called back, 'Wait, so you won't be here to make my coffee for weeks?'

She just laughed as he walked out, shaking his head as if this was the worst news that he could receive that day.

Regular customers knew she was taking two weeks off, but others who were regular but less chatty heard Michael call out to her when leaving and they too wished her a nice break. One quiet, older gentleman she knew as Tom told her she worked very hard and deserved a nice break. It was the most she had ever heard him speak in the months he had been coming in. Sally felt good; her boss might not appreciate her, but she knew her customers did.

She had planned to go to her mum's, pack up the albums in boxes very carefully, and load them into her car. When she got outside work, her dad was waiting for her, leaning up against his driver's door; he anticipated her reaction to him being there, waiting on her after work, so he give a big smile reserved only for his two girls and walked to meet her halfway.

'What's wrong, Daddy?'

'Nothing's wrong. Just stopped by to tell you I have been chatting to Mal. He called me today, pet.' John, never one to beat about the bush, continued, 'I told him straight if it's you he's looking to chat to, he better be ready to be up front, and if it's a relationship he wants, he better be willing to lay down his life for you.'

'Daddy!' she said, mortified. But then defrosting just as quick, she added, 'What did he say?'

'He said he's come back for you, pet. He's willing to give up everything to be with you, but he wanted my go-ahead before getting in touch with you.'

Sally's heart stopped beating, then beat hard and fast, then stopped again, as did her breath. 'Breathe, pet.' Her dad shook her slightly. Her heart swapped places with her tummy, and she thought she was about to throw them both up. She couldn't believe her ears.

'Tell me again, Daddy, please.' Her daddy told her again, word for word, while he held her in his arms for fear if he let go he would lose her in more ways than one . . .

When they got back to her parents' house, her mum was waiting patiently, haven't been filled in on the events as John drove to meet up with Sally.

'How are you feeling, darling?' she asked with more excitement in her voice than she intended. 'Must have been the flowers magic,' Elizabeth laughed, only half joking.

'Oh my God, Mum, what do I do? Am so nervous and excited, I can't breathe proper. I can't think straight.' Sally saw the bags packed on the living room sofa, ready to be transferred to the boot of their black A4; they were going to drive off and leave her in the middle of all this drama. She started to hyperventilate, well, slightly . . .

Elizabeth lifted the phone, walked to the other side of the room, chatted, laughed, and then walked back towards Sally and her dad, finishing the conversation, saying, 'And bring in one of those bottles of champagne we bought for Sligo.' Laughing, she hung up.

Twenty minutes later, Anna, Jim, Nicole, and Johnny were sitting at the kitchen island.

'Thank God, we weren't stopping for the Dale Farm concoction,' Anna said, rolling her eyes, a smile on her face and her glass in mid-air.

Everyone laughed, but Johnny just looked lost for a second until Nicole reminded him. They all clinked glasses in the mist of joy. Sally thought the only person missing was Mal; then she realised she didn't even know if her dad had passed on her number or how they had left things. Her tummy flipped as she asked him.

'I didn't give him your number, pet. I took his.'

'But I thought you already had it, Daddy?' she questioned, confused.

'I have two now, his Spanish mob, which he won't need any more, and his UK one. He's coming back to Derry, pet. Will be arriving tomorrow night . . .'

The room spun round and round; her heart, head, and tummy felt like they were playing musical chairs. The only thing that stopped her from falling to the floor in an emotional heap was Nicole screaming – deafening high-pitched screams. Even her dad, who never turned a word in his princess's mouth, told her to shush, in the most affectionate way he could, of course.

'I am taking over the franchise for cactus flowers,' she was screeching. 'Am going to be rich.' She clasped her hands in front of her heart.

Johnny was trying to explain that cactus plants weren't actually a franchise type of business in the most affectionate way he too could find.

John handed his emotional wreck of a daughter a yellow post-it; on it, it simply said 'Mal' and his number. Once again, for the hundredth time that week, her heart was ready to burst and was starting to win the fight with her head . . .

Elizabeth, John, Anna, and Jim set off for Sligo, after helping Sally load her boot with the albums. Johnny sat in the car, waiting for the girls to say their goodbyes. 'You would think they were parting for a year,' Johnny thought.

'You will see each other next week,' he called out the window.

Nicole rolled her eyes, saying, 'Boys just don't get it.'

They had arranged to visit Culdaff next week when they got back from visiting Johnny's parents in Letterkenny. Nicole always dreaded staying over, although she loved them to bits. Mr and Mrs White were very set in their ways. Both in their seventies, she was never without her apron nor he his cap. They grew their own vegetables and kept chickens in the yard. The teapot was always stewing on the hob, and the front door always open. They were pure country folk, and Nicole was like a beautiful whirlwind blowing through their cottage, Johnny would say when Nicole would mention not fitting in.

'So the ball's in your court now. When are you going to ring him?' Nicole asked.

'Do you not mean *am* I going to ring him?' Sally said with a knowing smile.

'Yeah, right! I hate that I am going to be stuck looking out at chickens and drinking stewed tea at a cottage in Letterkenny with seventy-year-olds, and you're going to be going through all this excitement without me,' Nicole said in a huffy voice, her bottom lip pushed out in a pout, but she was only joking half heartily; she wished nothing more than to be in the middle of all the drama.

'I think I will go to Culdaff and clear my head for a few days before I ring him. What do you think?' Sally wasn't sure what to do with the information she had just received. If someone would have asked her last week what she would do, she would have said, without a doubt, she would have rung the number on the spot. Reality was a lot different.

'Aye, I think that's a good idea. You will know yourself when you're ready to make the call. Are you bringing your cactus with you?'

'Yes, it will be the first thing I put in the car.' Sally laughed, rolling her eyes, and she kissed Nicole, then waved bye to Johnny.

'Don't forget I am home till Sunday morning,' Nicole reminded Sally, 'in case you have anything to inform me of.' She finished with eyes popping out of her head. Nicole was working right up until Saturday; it would be very busy at the salon, so her holidays were starting later than everyone else's, but she was taking the following week off.

Sally drove a half an hour to Carndonagh or Carn, as everyone called it, in a daze and the next ten minutes to Culdaff; she took in the beautiful houses and grounds around them, the little cottages that looked like time had forgotten them. The fields were filled with cows out for their first graze of grass this year, along with sheep and horses, all mixed in green pastures, not a care between them. She was already feeling lighter by the time she turned the key into the double doors of the mobile home. The smell of lemon instantly reminded her of her mum, and she knew she must have been down at some stage that week, cleaning and airing the place out for her. She hooked up the gas for the oven and fire. She switched on the water and made up the bed, bleached the toilets and sinks, and unloaded the car, taking great care with her cactus plant and her boxes of albums; she didn't want them to get mixed up and out of order. She poured a glass of wine and settled on a sun lounger on the decking with a citrus candle lit to keep the midges away. Looking out over the ocean, the view was something else; the clouds moved eastward and the big orange moon was shining through the red sky, which mirrored on the water and also told her it was to be a good day the next day. (Red sky at night is a sailor's delight.) It was so peaceful, and the third glass of wine went down as lovely as the first and second . . .

The next day was spent hiking up the mountain, not that Sally looked at it as hiking when she set out, but when she started up the steep road that led to the mountain, she was out of breath and she hadn't even set foot on the mossy grass trail on the mountain itself. When she reached the top where dead man's cave was, she decided she had definitely hiked a big mountain! She didn't remember it being this hard when she was younger. She didn't dare go close enough to the edge to see into the cave, not when she was alone up there. She sat as near as she dared to the mountain's edge and took in the views; she could see the outline of the lighthouse in the middle of the sea, more mountains, grass, sea and sky, and it was blissful.

On returning to the mobile, although she was shattered, she made a quick dinner of pasta and tuna and ate every bite, washing it down with a large glass of milk. She was surprised at how much she was at peace with her own company, and at night, with a bottle of wine in her, she enjoyed the craic with herself too.

On Saturday morning, when she woke, every muscle in her body hurt after her 'big mountain hike', so she decided to lay about in bed looking through the albums; she started with the first one in her mum's orderly pile. It was before she was born. Her mum and dad were only dating, and she looked so much like her mum; it was scary and flattering. The next album was their wedding album – beautiful photos, and both her grandparents were in them. She got up, made coffee, scrambled eggs and toast, and lay back on the bed; before she knew it was three o'clock, so she took a long hot shower; dried her hair out straight; applied body butter from head to toe; polished her nails, hands, and feet; applied her make-up; dressed in light denim skinny jeans and a white vest top, slightly wedged beige sandals, and a coral oversized cardigan; and dandered to the guesthouse just in the road; it took her ten minutes to walk to it. It had a lovely restaurant or you could eat pup grub in the bar. Sally was going to find a quiet table in the pub, order dinner, and people-watch. Hopefully, she wouldn't stand out like a sore thumb dining on her own.

Chapter 7

'Jaysus Mary Joseph and the wee donkey, look who it is,' Nicole said, calmer than she felt.

Mal Quinn was standing in the waiting room of her salon, and she could bet her life it wasn't a coincidence. She walked towards him with scissors and comb in her hand, leaving the girl whose hair she was cutting without a word, not taking her eyes off Mal.

'You're not really coming at me with those scissors now, Nic,' Mal laughed but had the confidence of a lion leading his pride.

'You look well,' Nicole managed to say. He bent and kissed her cheek and gave her a hug. She took in his jet-black hair, tanned, toned skin, and darkest brown eyes. He did look well, and Sally would think so too. 'She would bloody combust,' Nicole thought to herself.

'Where is she, Nic?' His voice was friendly but commanding.

'She's gone to the mobile for a break over Easter,' she blurted out with no filter from brain to mouth.

'Culdaff?' Mal asked, a note of triumph in his voice.

'Look, Mal, give her a few days. Johnny and I are going down next week, Tuesday or Wednesday. If you like, you could travel down with us.' Nicole was talking a mile a minute now.

Mal narrowed his eyes, a horrible thought filling his head. Is it possible Nic was panning him off because Sal wasn't alone? 'Is she with someone? In Culdaff, I mean.'

'No, no, of course not, that's not what I am saying, Mal. It's just it was a big shock hearing you're back after ten years, you know?'

'I won't keep you, Nic. You're busy.' He turned on his heels, and with extreme satisfaction on his face he added 'Catch you later, Nic.'

'Will you wait and go down with us on Tuesday or Wednesday, whatever day suits you?' Panic was settling in Nicole's voice.

But Mal just replied, 'Aye, no bother.'

Nicole pushed a business card from the reception counter into his hand, and he was gone, leaving her ready to explode with excitement and frustration. It was twelve noon; the salon was so busy she could hardly get a lunch break. How the hell was she going to get through the rest of the day, never mind the trip to Letterkenny with tea, chickens, aprons, and an old man in a cap that didn't talk much? 'Jaysus,' she said out loud, louder than she intended . . .

Chapter 8

It was seven o'clock when Sally was paying her bill and leaving the bar; she had just eaten the freshest cod she had ever tasted with chips and tartar sauce and drunk sparkling water with her dinner; then she had a glass of red wine while she people-watched, not that there were many to watch. The bar was spacious with plenty of seating and a pool table where two teenage boys played while two girls of similar age giggled and chewed gum at a table near them. As she was leaving, it started to fill with people out for the evening. All ages and dress sense were welcome, obviously. She dandered back in the road, noticing a red car parked behind the mobile home next to hers. 'Must be Mr and Mrs Mc Williams,' she thought, as she passed the Mc Williams's mobile. She was having a wee nosey through their mobile window, she didn't see the car door open, but she certainly saw who got out . . .

Six feet four inches of Mal Quinn in the flesh. She stopped as if she had hit an invisible screen. She took in every inch of him – his dark hair falling, slightly long over his forehead, slightly long on the back and sides too, tanned skin that made him look even more Spanish than he had before, nearly black eyes with thick lashes fanning his face, as he too scanned her over from head to toe. He had a labour's build, bulky and toned; he was definitely not the boy that had left for Spain ten years ago, but Sally's heart thumped in her chest just the same, if not stronger now. His long legs were clad in light denim, like hers, and a black T-shirt fitted like a second skin to his muscular body. She wanted to say something, but her head was candy floss and her mouth like a fur boot; she swallowed over but couldn't get a greeting together in her head. Mal just spoke her name and opened his arms wide, and she took a few steps into them and melted there . . .

His smell was sweet but masculine, and she wanted to rub her cheek against his chest to relish more, so she did. She felt his tight chest expand as he breathed her in too. His grip grew tighter as did hers. God knows how long they stayed embracing like they did, totally intoxicated; neither of them wanted to let go, in case they woke from their dream. When Sally lifted her chin slightly to look up at him, he held her tight but pulled his head back to look down at her.

'How did you know where to find me?' she asked softly.

'Nic,' he answered, a wide smile showing off his white teeth, still with the tiniest wee gap between his front two bottom ones. 'Nic is going to feed drama off this for a long time,' he said, smiling fondly.

Sally smiled too. 'Oh, so you remember her well then?'

They both stared at each other in disbelief, then dropped their hands in front of them but still held on; she nodded towards the mobile. 'Coming in?'

'Got custard creams?' he asked.

Inside, she couldn't believe how easy it was to walk back into his arms, but she still had one thing niggling at her when they settled on the sofa with tea for Mal, coffee for Sally, and a plate of custard creams. She asked him the question that had been breaking her heart all these years.

'Why didn't you write to me, Mal?'

'I did, Sal, I swear. I wrote every weekend for the first six months and every once and a while after that for five years.'

Sally felt herself getting a bit angry, thinking he was going to start lying to make himself look better. He interrupted her thoughts, saying, 'My mum died a year ago, Sal. She was a great mum. I loved her so much and she loved me. It's the only reason for . . .,' he stumbled, so she put her coffee down and took his hands in hers. This gave him the strength to carry on. 'She would call me for work every morning at seven o'clock, even knowing I had my own alarm clock. On a Monday morning, she always said, "Leave your letter on the kitchen table, and I will post it with mine."' He dropped his head into his hands and rubbed at his face. Sally could see this conversation was hard for him to have. 'When she died, Sal, I had no one else in my life. I missed her so much, you know?' Sal didn't know what it was like to miss a parent like that, but she sure knew what it was like to miss someone she loved, so she nodded as much to answer him as to encourage him to continue. 'It took me months to get the courage to sort out her stuff. I found the letters I wrote to you, Sal, all bundled together in a plastic container.' He handed her a letter. 'This was at the top of the pile.'

Sorry. I couldn't risk you going back.
I love you.

Mama.

Sally could feel tears escape down her cheek one at a time. She couldn't believe it. He *had* written to her. It was a comfort to hear that. She would deal with her feelings about his mum later, she decided. She was dead now, after all. She couldn't speak; she was in shock. He reached up and put both his hands on each side of her face, wiping her tears away with his thumb.

'I need to kiss you, Sal.' And without waiting for an answer, he took her mouth with his in the most beautiful, soft, loving motion. His lips were soft and full, and she was once again melting in his arms. Her hands went to his face as his slid down to her waist to slide her closer to him; he didn't want a hair's breadth between them ever again. They kissed until they were both breathless and their lips were swollen. When his lips were finished with hers, for now, he stared into her eyes with the sincerest look on his face.

'For ten years, I thought you hated me, thought you didn't care or want me in your life, but please don't hate my mother. She was a great but lonely woman.' He kissed her again before she could answer. Parting lips again, he added, 'Mother's parents died within four months of each other just a year after we moved there. It was the worst two years of my life, Sal. I didn't have you. My mother was so busy with my grandparents. She tried so hard to look after everyone. I was never so lonely. Then after the death of her parents, she became clingy with me. When I came home from work, she would have a feast ready. She would near beg me to sit with her and talk about my day. If I said I was going out, ye know to the pub or something, she would suddenly feel unwell.'

Sally's tears fell afresh; all this time she'd thought he'd forgotten about her, that he was off having a great time with a busload of beautiful Spanish girls. All this time, he was going through hell. 'Am so, so sorry, Mal.'

He kissed her again, not able to fight the urge to taste her sweet lips; he decided there and then he loved her drinking red wine. He could taste it with every dip of his tongue. He never wanted to stop tasting Sally Mc Quire on his lips ever again . . .

That night was spent kissing, cuddling, and chatting, and before they knew it, it was four in the morning. The natural light started to make its way in through the break in the curtains as the sun rose on a new day, a day they hadn't yet rested for, but a new day with Mal Quinn in it was sounding like a dream – a dream she thought she would only ever dream, not actually live . . .

'Bedtime,' Sally announced. 'I mean, not like us, just like you go . . . I go. I . . . I . . . I will make up the room for you.' She turned to hide the embarrassment of the misunderstanding that she might have been asking him into her bed already. Jeez, they never ever had sex. *She* never ever had sex. They had never even talked about it and for him to think that on the first night back together she would offer it on a plate; she was beyond red-faced. He pulled her by the arm and into his lap. She fell on him with a surprised girlie squeal; he bent her right back, took her mouth again for seconds, pulled his head back, kissed her nose, and said, 'Sal, I've waited ten years. I will wait again as long as I know you are by my side.'

Sally woke the next morning at ten forty; she couldn't believe the time she had slept until, well, until she remembered the time they had sat up until; it was nearer five by the time they had stopped kissing again and made up the room next to Sally's. Another quick kiss and they bid goodnight and went to separate beds – reluctantly!

She was pulled from her memory of the night before by the sound of music playing and what sounded like Mal whistling to a tune. She got up, checked herself in the mirror for mascara goop and panda eyes, ruffled her hair, straightened her vest top and boy-short PJs, and thanked the love gods above, the cactus flower, and the flower that Nicole had planted (she couldn't remember the name) that she had shaved her legs the evening before. Taking a deep breath and letting it out again, she walked out to the sight of a very bare-chested Mal cooking a fry-up, wearing loose-fitting grey jammies with green dollar signs printed all over them, his feet bare, bum tight and rounded, muscles on show, arms tight, chest rippling, shoulders, back, and front bulging, and she was his only audience, for now. He still didn't know she was salivating behind him, drinking in the most beautiful view in Culdaff to date. He was now singing along to Robin Thicke's 'Blurred Lines', but Robin Thicke had sweet nothing on Mal Quinn, standing near naked in her parents' luxury mobile home, cooking her breakfast. 'God,' she thought, 'he knows full well what he's doing standing here looking like that.'

She walked towards him, joining in the song at 'You're the hottest bitch in this place'.

He started slightly at the interruption, then said, 'That you are, beautiful.' He held her hand, dwarfing it in his, wrapped his other around her waist, and dipped for the kiss he was waiting on all morning from the minute he had woken.

She pulled back slightly. 'Bitch?' She raised one eyebrow, asking jokingly.

'Hot.' Kiss. 'Beautiful.' *kiss*

'Sexy.' *kiss*

'Precious.' *kiss*

'Bitch? No.' He shook his head slowly. *kiss*

'Mine? Yes.' He nodded. *kiss*

'Fry-up?'

This time it was Sally who was nodding and said, 'yes', in a very breathy infatuated state.

They ate and chatted about his work in Spain. He was in partnership with a Spanish bloke in a handmade garden furniture company that was thriving. He had organised through solicitors in Spain to become a silent partner indefinitely. He didn't want to give up the business but planned to set up the same style of company here also, making handmade furniture to order. He predicted the bestsellers would be the children's bedroom furniture with their favourite characters and names carved in them. He was so passionate about his work; she felt herself picturing him working, muscles bulging and bare tanned skin on show . . . 'Concentrate on the conversation,' Sally told herself. ('And they slag men for talking to women's breasts,' she thought with a smile). When they had finished their breakfast and loaded the dishwasher, they took a walk to the small beach in front of the site.

'We used to call this our own private beach,' she told him, 'because years ago, anyone coming to Culdaff stopped at the park in the road and went to the beach in there. The people from the site had this beach all to themselves.'

'Not so now?' he asked, listening to every bit of information he could absorb from her about her.

Because the tide was out, they could walk the length of both the small beaches, divided only by rocks. Sally's arms were wrapped around his waist, with her joined at his side and her head tucked under his arm, resting on the side of his chest. He had his arm around her shoulders, brushing her hair from her face every now and again to see her eyes when she looked up to him to talk. They looked and felt every bit a couple in love.

They sat on a grassy hilltop between the small beaches. She sat between his long legs with his long arms wrapped around her like a fleece blanket. A comfortable silence fell between them as they sat contentedly holding each other. Breaking the silence first, it was Mal who spoke, 'Did you ever meet anyone else, Sal? Anyone you really liked?'

She sighed deeply and answered honestly, 'No. There were a few boyfriends, but none ever lasted longer than a month or so. How about you?'

'Same as you,' he replied with relief on hearing her reply. 'I never got much of a chance with Mother being the way she was. I had a few girlfriends, if that's what you would even call them, but nothing steady or serious.'

Sally was equally relieved at his response. She looked out over the blue sea meeting with the blue sky and watched the white horses crash on the sandy beach; it was picture perfect, and she spoke from her heart, 'Looks like we were waiting for each other. It's like our hearts always knew we were going to be together, but our minds wouldn't dare let us dream.'

He held her tight, and moving her to one side, he said, 'I couldn't have put it better myself.' *kiss*

'I love you, Sal.' *kiss*

'I always have.' *kiss*

'And always will.' *kiss*

She kissed him back with so much love for him she thought she was going to explode. She turned herself in between his legs without breaking the kiss until she could face him, on her knees and at eye level.

One hand went to her heart as if it were a magnet and the other went to the back of his neck, holding him as she said the three little words she swore she would never say again to anyone, let alone dream she would have a chance of saying them to Mal Quinn.

'I love you.' She couldn't help herself, so she said them again, 'I love you, Mal. I always have and always will.' Then with fake alarm, 'Wait, I forgot to kiss you in between each declaration.'

He rolled her on to the grass and snogged the life *into* her over and over again.

Chapter 9

Nicole was beside herself. Poor Johnny's head was done in, listening to her go on and on about Mal Quinn turning up at her salon. She tried to tell Johnny's mum the story. Nicole was so excited telling her that Mrs White tried but found it hard to keep up with her.

They had driven to Letterkenny on Sunday morning, taking Easter eggs for Mr and Mrs White, knowing full well they would not be eaten, but it was more a token of the holiday. Nicole never devalved from the minute Johnny picked her up from work the night before. They cooked dinner together that night, with Nicole only taking a breath from talking about the 'prodigal lover' to sip her wine and chew her steak and veg when it was served and put in front of her. The more wine she drank, the dreamier she became, fantasising about the upcoming week.

'We will pull into the site, park the car. Sally will come running out to hug me but will run into Mal's arms instead. Oh, it's going to be so sweet, Johnny. And we will be there to witness everything.' She was swaying as she spoke. Johnny wasn't sure it was the dreamy state she was in or the wine; he just smiled looking at her and listening. It was exactly why he loved her so much, and it was exactly why he had to make his proposal the most romantic scene, which even she herself couldn't dream up. 'That'll be a challenge,' he laughed to himself. 'She's in a constant dreamworld.'

Nicole's mind was on overdrive by Monday morning. Mal hadn't rung her, and she couldn't understand why. If he was as keen as he seemed, she expected him to ring before now. She ran through her conversation with him one more time with Johnny, and as she got to the part of giving him the 'business card' off the counter in the salon, Johnny caught on to the fact that Nicole's salon number was on the card, not her mobile. Flying into a blind panic, she called herself all the stupid animals she could think of.

'OK, OK, let's get packed up and head home,' said Johnny, knowing Nicole couldn't manage another moment of not being able to put her head together with Sally's and ponder over everything that'd happened and could happen. She leapt into his arms in delight at not having to make that same suggestion. He carried her to their room with her both legs wrapped around his waist, as she gave him tiny kisses up and down his face and neck. He threw her gently on the bed and told her to get packing. 'We have a dilemma to attend to, sweet cheeks,' he tossed over his shoulder as he went to find his mum in the kitchen and let her know they were leaving.

They stopped at Bridgend for lunch; Johnny was starving and talked Nicole into it, saying it would save time in the long run because he wouldn't have to cook something when he got home and then clean up. They went home, unpacked, packed again, and were on their way to Culdaff by five o'clock. Sally's mobile phone would only work if she was in Culdaff town, so there was no point ringing, but Nicole sent a text anyway.

On r way c u soon xxxx

Sally's Monday morning started the same as Sunday morning had; this time instead of a fry-up, it was poached eggs and toast, and instead of Robin Thicke's 'Blurred Lines', it was Tom Jones's 'Sex Bomb'. 'Very apt,' Sally announced, entering the kitchen and kissing Mal's shoulder. She could feel his breath catch as the contact affected him, so she kissed the other shoulder, only to be lifted off her feet to come up eye level and get a delicious warm kiss . . .

After breakfast, Sally produced some albums, telling Mal all about her mum putting them together and how she had brought them with her, thinking she would be halfway through them by now, but the distraction was very welcome, she added. Mal left Sally to her albums, braving the ocean for a swim.

Sally had a laugh to herself, looking at the old photos and remembering days out, birthday parties of hers or her mum's or dad's;

her jaws were sore from smiling and her back was sore as she slummed over the low coffee table in the living area. She decided on a break; stretching herself as she stood, she went and ran a shower. She washed her hair, shaved her bits (de-fuzzed herself as Nicole would say), and body-buttered herself from head to foot; she dried her hair, leaving it wavy instead of blow-drying it straight, then lay on top of the bed with the towel still wrapped around her and fell asleep.

Mal was quite refreshed after his swim in the ocean, and he headed back to the mobile, having missed Sally even knowing he was only gone an hour or so. He was thinking about her emerald eyes and wide smile; the effect they had on him ten years ago was nothing to what it did to him now. She wasn't in and he felt disappointed; he could nearly feel her in his arms, smiling up at him with those glistening green emeralds of hers, the closer he got to the door of the mobile home.

He went for a shower to rid himself of the salt on his skin; as he soaped himself up in the hot shower, he thought of where Sally could have got to. Her car was still parked outside. The albums were still spread across the coffee table. She must have gone for a walk, he decided.

He wrapped a small towel around his private parts (just about), drying his hair with the only other small towel he could find in the en-suite. He walked towards the kitchen for a drink of water. He stopped in his tracks when he saw Sally standing there in a towel, not much bigger than his own, and having a tough time covering her private parts. His eyes stung at the sight of so much of her beautiful silky skin; he loved her wavy hair, and the way it fell on her bare shoulders was just an invite to nibble the flesh under it. He felt his blood run fast and his self-control disintegrated within seconds. Her eyes glazed over as she looked down his glowing, hard bare body and up again to his hooded eyes; she knew what she saw in them, and she hoped he would see the same in hers. She wanted him and couldn't deny herself any longer. She had waited her whole adult life for him, for this moment.

'I fell asleep after my shower.' Her voice was husky.

She watched him walk, like a panther, slowly towards her.

'You did?' he said as he reached out, his heart pounding in his ears, and there was also a pounding that he could not control any longer between his legs. He lifted her by the waist, his arms trapping her to his rock-hard body. 'You look beautiful, Sal.' Her words escaped her brain. She couldn't think; she could only feel – feelings that were all too long coming. 'Too beautiful, Sal.' He shook his head. She knew he was silently telling her he couldn't wait any more than she could. They still just stared, from each other's starving eyes to their eager mouths. 'Are we still waiting, Sal?' He held her up with one arm as he cupped her chin with his other.

'No,' she said, shaking her head; she didn't know if it were her tears that were choking her or her heart. Her body was shaking with excitement. She had to have him, every inch of Mal Quinn; they'd waited long enough. 'Take me to bed, Mal. Please . . .'

Chapter 10

By five o'clock that evening, they had only left Sally's bed once – for water. They didn't plan on leaving it any time soon either. Only their bellies were protesting; they hadn't eaten anything since their poached eggs and toast that morning. After Mal joked he was going to tie her to the bed so she could not get out of his sight ever again, they decided to eat in. They showered separately after trying to squeeze into the cubicle together with no luck; the showers in the mobile were compact and barely big enough for Mal on his own. They gave it up as a bad job. Even while cooking dinner, they couldn't keep their hands off each other. He would squeeze her ass as she chopped peppers or kiss her neck when draining rice; he was in charge of the chicken in the pan, and when he was flipping and stirring, she stood so close to him, leaning over his arms to look in the pan, rubbing her breasts on his forearms, teasing him, flirting with him with her body and eyes. He knew exactly what she was doing. He caught her by the wrists; he couldn't control himself any longer, and he held both her wrists in one hand, flicking the gas switch to turn the chicken off with his other. She was giggling at him, trying to back away.

'You're in for it now, my sweet Sal.' He scooped her up over his shoulder and swatted her backside. She let out a yelp, and he made towards the bedroom they had just left forty minutes ago. Just as he reached the door, Nicole came bouncing through the double doors, her mouth on the mat at her feet.

'Jaysus Mary and joooo . . . what the hell?'

'What's the craic?' Johnny's voice came from behind her, edging in past a stunned Nicole, carrying an overnight bag. Sally was both excited to see Nicole and Johnny and disappointed she didn't make it back through the bedroom door that was now behind her back as Mal stood her down.

Throwing his arm over Sally's shoulder, Mal said, 'All right, Nic?' He stretched his other arm out to shake hands with Johnny.

'Oh, this is Mal. Mal, meet Johnny,' Sally said, realising the men had never met before and, for a split second, hoping they'd get on together.

Nicole's drama kicked in, and she threw herself at the lovebirds, trying to hug them together; then just hugging Sally as tight as she could, she whispered in her ear, 'Am so delighted for you, Sally.'

They all sat at the kitchen table, and Mal suggested they eat dinner with Sally and him, saying he had enough chicken on to feed them all, and he would put on a few oven chips for extras. While Mal finished the cooking, Sally poured wine for Nicole and herself, and Johnny got the case of beer from the boot of his car for the boys.

'Mal, did you ever ring the number on the card Nicole gave you, you know for a lift down here with us?' Johnny said, winking at Sally.

Sally was confused but was all ears. Nicole dropped her head into her hands, giggling. Mal was smiling with a confused look on his face, looking from Nicole to Johnny, but answered, 'Naw, man, I just headed straight for my girl. Why?'

Laughing and rubbing Nicole's shoulders at the same time, Johnny told him he would have been in for a long wait, as the salon was closed until Thursday and it was the only number on the card. Nicole put her head back into her hands, embarrassed.

'I was in a blind panic, and I didn't want *him* barging down here if you weren't ready to see him.' Nicole was wagging a finger at Mal as she spoke to Sally with a voice full of genuine concern. 'But he barged anyway,' Nicole said the last bit with a mock stern look directed at Mal again.

'Sorry, Nic, but I waited long enough for her.'

'Umm, you're forgiven, Mal Quinn.' She squinted at him like a ten-year-old. Mal filled Nicole and Johnny in with a short version of the story; Sally listened to it again, as if hearing it for the first time. She still could not believe this weekend wasn't a dream she was in.

Nicole was in a state of dreaminess again and kept saying either 'Oh my God' or 'Are you serious' or 'I can't believe it' or 'It's all sooo romantic'.

Dinner was ready – chicken strips in rice, veg, and a homemade salsa sauce with a big bowl of freshly tossed salad and oven chips in the centre of the table so they could help themselves. Sally was listening to the carefree chatter of the foursome; it was so amazing sitting having dinner with Nicole and Johnny and Mal by her side, who was squeezing her leg every now and then, even going a bit further up at one stage, which made her yelp just as the smack on her butt had done when Mal had thrown her over his shoulder earlier. She had to let on; she choked on a piece of chicken and coughed into her shoulder, looking up at Mal with wide eyes. He just had mischief in his.

The boys cleaned up, although Mal did most of the cooking. The girls retired to the decking with refilled glasses. Nicole couldn't wait to get Sally on her own, and Sally had a feeling Johnny was given 'a look' that said, 'You keep him occupied in here. I will see to her out there.' When they lit the citrus candles and got cosy on the sun loungers, Nicole leant in and said, 'I say we have ten minutes, so go, spill.'

'Oh my God, Nicole, can you believe it?' Sally started. 'He was just standing there when I came back from the pub, getting dinner. I was in shock, but as soon as he opened up his arms, without a word even spoken, Nicole, I just walked into them.'

The two girls squealed, kicking their bare feet up and down on the foot of the sun loungers like teenagers, laughing their heads off at themselves, with Sally shushing Nicole.

Mal and Johnny were talking shop while cleaning up. Mal was telling Johnny about his plans to settle back in Derry, to open his own furniture business here, and Johnny being an estate agent said he would keep an eye out for properties for him. They were discussing his needs when they heard the girls squealing; Johnny never flinched. Mal's eyes went like saucers freezing on the spot. When he looked at Johnny, he just shook his head at him with a 'don't go there' look on his face. The boys laughed too, knowing full well what their girls were gossiping about. They finished up in the kitchen, grabbed a couple of fresh, cold beers, and joined the girls on the decking.

'This is the life,' Johnny sighed, rubbing his cheek along Nicole's bare neck and shoulders. She was resting back into his body as they shared the sun lounger.

Mal sat on a deck chair and pulled Sally's feet on to his lap, rubbing them with one hand and drinking his beer with the other, saying, 'I'll drink to that man.' He had never felt so content. He had a few mates in Madrid, but he'd never taken the time to get to know them really. Building his business was his main aim in life back in Spain; back in Derry, life would be different. He was adamant to make a life with Sally, to make her happy and spend the rest of his life making up for the last ten years they had lost out on. He had to make it work with her, and he knew it would, because they were meant to be together. That's the reason he spoke to John first; he knew how much Sally's parents meant to her, and he wanted to be part of all their lives. Making sure John knew the full story and just how much Sally meant to him was the first step. Thankfully, John heard him out and wished him luck. He wanted 'this' right now, his girl by his side and the company of good friends. Sally looked so happy he wanted to memorise her face right now and always make her this happy, if not even more so. When he thought about going to bed that night, knowing he would be waking up in the morning with Sally Mc Quire in his arms for the first time, he actually got a bit nervous and excited, feelings that were all new to him, and he couldn't wait for more of the same. They sat chatting for another hour until it got too cold to sit on the decking. When they all got up to go inside, picking up the empty beer bottles and tops and blowing out the candles, he stayed Sally with his hand on her arm.

'I am so happy, Sal.' *kiss*

'You make me so happy.' *kiss*

'Right back at you, babe,' she replied and then . . . *kiss*

'Get a room,' Nicole called out.

'OK,' Mal said quickly and lifted her over his shoulder even quicker and started towards their bedroom door. Sally thought he was joking, but he definitely was not by the look in his eyes when he lowered her on to the floor.

'You will have to make up your own bed, Nicole,' Sally shouted out through the thin walls.

'Hope you have earplugs,' Mal shouted too, not moving his eyes from Sally's.

Sally was mortified and shouted at him in disbelief but still giggling, 'Mal.'

Nicole's face must have been a picture, because all they could hear was Johnny's laughter . . .

Chapter 11

The following day was damp and much cooler, so they decided after breakfast to look at the albums. Then Sally pulled out an album titled 'Summer 2004'. She knew it was her and Mal's year; she had been looking forward to flicking through it with him. Had she been here in Culdaff on her own, she would have avoided it, either that or driven straight to the town for a signal on her phone to ring him. So she gave Nicole and Johnny the album 'Winter/Xmas 2004', which probably had pictures of her and Mal too, but it was the summer one she really wanted to cuddle up with Mal to flick through, so she sat between his long legs, lengthways on the sofa, her head resting back against his chest and the album resting against her thighs. The very first page had three photos, one of her, all moody looking, standing in front of the Molly Malone statue in Dublin; it was the Easter break before they had started going out. The second one was of her mum and dad in front of the Floozie in the Jacuzzi. (It was a nickname given to a huge statue of a lady with really long hair lying in a huge pool which doubled for a fountain. She never did know the reason for her, and she is not there now. The Dubs must have thought against it because of her nickname maybe.) The third was of the three of them outside the GPO on O'Connell Street. The next few were much of the same, photos of the three of them at Dublin zoo and their hotel bedroom and lobby. Then she came to a page of two photos, both of Mal and her on their very first date to the bowling alley. When Mal had called at the door for her that night dressed in jeans, a polo shirt, and a pair of Converse, her dad had insisted on leaving them to the bowling alley and then collecting them again. The first photo was of them at the front door on their way out.

They had stood about twenty inches apart, both joining their hands in front of their bodies, fingers entwined nervously, heads dipped, not a smile in sight. The second was when they returned to Sally's house; it was still early enough. Sally's parents never liked her hanging about places, so 'there and back' was their motto. Mal was allowed back for 'an hour' just. Her mum got the camera out again and did an unconscious before and after picture. They sat on the green plastic 'love seat' in the back garden. They didn't know the picture was being taken until the flash went. Mal sat with one arm along the back of the seat, turned to the side to face Sally, one leg tucked under the other; he was laughing, leaning towards her, and Sally's head was dropped slightly, smoothing her top out on her lap, but it was still clear she was laughing too. They looked a lot more comfortable in this picture. They flicked through lots more, like one of them holding hands, walking down the driveway; her mum had called their names, and they had both turned into each other to look back, still holding hands. Picnics and BBQs, walks in St Columb's Park, some with just them and some with Nicole and Brian, family photos, and friendship photos – they were just amazing to look at again and made more amazing by the fact that she was doing so in Mal's arms. Sally actually felt herself become overwhelmed, she was so happy. Tears didn't fall, but she was very emotional. They laughed and giggled at the photos, and when Nicole or Sally saw an extra hilarious one, they would shriek 'Oohhh look, look, look' or 'Awww, please don't look at that one' or 'it was "*all in*" back then'. They had a really enjoyable wee morning, but Nicole felt sorry for Johnny; he must have been bored (not that Johnny would ever say), so she offered to make a light lunch of sandwiches and asked Johnny to drive her into town for supplies.

'I can't believe your mum kept all these photos, Sal. They are a class to look back at,' Mal said, and she could hear the wonder in his voice. 'My mum got rid of all the photos of us as a family when she and Dad split up. These are so precious, Sal.'

'I know.' Sally had always known they were, but in that moment, she realised just how much.

'I want to take you out tonight for a meal. What do you think?' Mal kind of asked; it was more of a confirmation than a question, but she didn't mind one bit. He sat on a chair in the dining area, while she stood between his legs; his arms were caressing over her bum and up her spine, back down her thighs and a sneaky wee stroke between her legs now and again while he looked up at her, chatting as if nothing at all was occurring between them and between their legs.

She was going to try her very best to play *and* beat him at his own game, so she smiled sweetly and said, 'I better go and find something to wear then.' As she walked away and turned at the bedroom door, she saw him watch her, slightly deflated but still hopeful, and in her most seductive voice that she herself had never heard before, she added, 'I might need some help getting in and *out* of some things.'

Before she finished, he had leapt from the dining chair; the noise of the legs scraping against the wooden floor was all she heard through his laughter and her giggling.

'Minx,' he said, slapping her ass . . .

Nicole and Johnny decided to go on into Carn rather than Culdaff town for the supplies, so it took them three times as long. Deliberate, of course. When they got back, the sun had come out again and the air had got warmer. The tarmac had steam rising off it because of the heat drying the rain; the smell of damp grass heating up was a strong scent in the cloggy air. Mal and Sally sat on the decking as if they had been there the whole time, waiting on their sandwiches. Nicole made chicken salad, ham salad, doorstep sandwiches with the freshest of loaves that she herself cut into two-inch thick slices.

'A light lunch, Nicole?' Sally asked when she saw the feast which included a side of crisps. 'It looks delicious,' she added.

'Pity there's nowhere down here we could work all this food off on our roller boots,' Nicole complained.

'Roller boots?' asked Mal, looking from Sally to Nicole.

'Here,' said Johnny, passing Mal his iPhone with about ten photos of the girls up at the quay in their roller boots. Arms and leg everywhere, some they had posed for; the others were definitely action photos with faces and arms blurred slightly, because they were in motion, be it intentional or not.

Mal shook his head, laughing. 'I guess I will have to get used to you two and your wacky ways', he put an arm around Sally's waist, 'if I am going to be sticking around . . .' *kiss*

'Yeah, good luck with that,' said Johnny, nodding at the girls. 'I don't think ye ever get used to it. Ye never know what's next with those two. Tell him about the cactus.'

Sally went beetroot red; Nicole got so excited, clapping her hands a mile a minute in front of her face, she didn't even notice. Without taking a breath, Nicole filled Mal in on her wonderful magical plant that had brought him right back into Sally's arms. Mal laughed and thanked Nicole, checking out the magical plant on the sideboard.

'And by the way, Johnny White', she flung her arms around his neck, giving him quick little kisses all over his face, 'you wouldn't have me any other way, baby.'

'No, I wouldn't, sweet cheeks. Now go wash up, and we can go for a swim in the sea.'

'Ha, dream on, lover boy, your marigolds are under the sink,' she replied, a joke with a jag!

The radio was turned up full while the boys filled the dishwasher and cleaned down the kitchen. The girls tidied up too, making beds, cleaning the en-suites, hovering and dusting. All cleaning done, they got ready for a swim; well, the girls said they would stick to paddling. When they got to the beach, the boys stripped off to shorts and wasted no time in getting under the waves, their teeth chattering as they beckoned the girls in.

'Maybe in a bit,' Nicole lied. They had no intention of getting in above their knees.

The boys came out together and passed them as they headed towards their clothes, saying they were heading for the bottled water that they had brought with them already. The girls stayed at the edge, chatting and paddling; the next thing they knew, the boys, at the same time, lifted them from behind by the waist and ran full force into the sea. The girls squealed in protest, slapping and kicking to no avail. Before they knew it, they were seeing a blur of water, seaweed, and arms and legs under the sea. The pain of the freeze went straight to their hearts.

'Bastards,' Sally shouted through her shaking jaw and chattering teeth.

Nicole was shouting something about not having her Protect and Perfect Shampoo and Conditioner with her, and the boys were doubled over at the waist, laughing their heads off.

'Revenge will be sweet!' Sally threatened, trying her best to hold an angry face but losing that battle.

Chapter 12

Back at the mobile, after they had their showers and the girls had washed and perfected their hair and make-up they were soon ready for their night at Mc Gory's Hotel in Culdaff for a meal. They had three cars with them altogether, so they decided Mal would drive his rental into town and they would take a taxi back. The next day, Johnny would drive Mal back into town to pick his car up.

Sally didn't get to choose something to wear earlier, but she decided on red skinny jeans and a black sleeveless lace high-neck blouse that rested on her hips. Her hair fell in soft blonde waves and rested on her shoulders; she borrowed the black wedges of Nicole, and she was set to go.

Nicole, as always, took the longest, even though she was the first in the shower. She wore a racing car green and gold maxi dress that made the auburn of her hair shine like her personality and lots of gold jewellery.

When Mal came into the bedroom to get his watch from the bedside locker, he made Sally jump; she was concentrating on getting the back on her earring and didn't hear him come in.

'Aww, Jaysus, baby, you're killing me,' he said, coming up behind her, grinding at her. 'Your ass is sweet in those jeans.'

'Mal, you better stop or we won't make it to dinner.'

'We might not make it out of this bedroom, baby,' he said, pulling back her hair to expose her shoulders for him to nibble on.

'I didn't plan on being an appetiser,' giggled Sally.

'Aggrrr,' he growled, still nibbling.

'But I do plan on being dessert,' she teased.

'Awww.' He fell back on the bed. 'You are going to make me uncomfortable all night,' he said, adjusting his jeans at the crotch.

'Up you get or you will crease your shirt,' she scolded him. She pulled him up by the hand and smoothed his shirt over his tight shoulders. 'You look hot and very sexy in that shirt.' He wore blue jeans, blue Converse (different pair from the first date), and a crisp white shirt with the shirt sleeves rolled up a little bit and the first few buttons undone (not Simon Cowell undone, just Mal Quinn undone). It was so sexy on him she couldn't wait to ogle him all night: to watch his tight ass walk to the bar or the toilets and walk right back to her again. He kissed her softly on the lips, lingering for a moment.

'Here.' He took his hand out of his pocket and produced a chain, unboxed, and she looked from him to the chain. He had never left her side since he arrived. When could he have bought her this? She scooped it up; it was beautiful. Its gold links were larger than your usual chain but still delicate, and it had a gold Celtic cross attached to it. She knew, looking at it, that it wasn't new, not because it was worn but because it had something about it, something she couldn't quite explain, but she felt it. 'It was my ma's, Sal. I want you to have it.' He lifted it from her hand, scooped her hair round to fall down one side, and attached it round her neck, kissing her on both cheeks, then her lips. 'I don't know much about the chain, but my ma had it for as long as I can remember and was never without it. I don't mean for you to wear it like that, but I wanted you to have it, Sal.'

'I love it. I love you so much you make my heart ache for more of you, and I never want to be without you ever again,' Sally gushed, holding the cross with one hand, her other caressing his cheek.

kiss kiss kiss

Bang bang bang

'Are you two ready?' called Nicole.

'Is this relationship always going to have four in it?' whispered Mal in her ear as she called out, 'Coming.'

'Jesus, again?' came Johnny's voice.

Then Nicole squealed. 'Jonathan Cain White!' She shouted, 'Mal, you're a bad influence on my boyfriend.'

Sally's mouth fell open, and her hand flew up to it.

'What'd I do?' Mal asked, coming through the door with a look of pure innocence on his face.

'We will wait in the car for you two. Keys please?' Nicole put one hand on her hip and the other stretched out in front of her, but she wouldn't make eye contact with him. Mal dangled the keys in front of her, and when she reached for them, he yanked them back.

'Smile, Nic. You will give yourself early wrinkles.'

'Maaaallll, you're soooo annoying.' And she whipped the keys from him and pretended to punch his tummy, and he pretended to go on his knees.

Sally ruffled his hair, walking past him. 'Let's go.'

He stood and slapped her ass, grumbling, 'Can't wait to peel those jeans off you later.'

'You have no shame.' She swatted his hand away from her bum playfully as she locked up.

Mal walked to the bar, his sexy ass on show, as if he knew what Sally was looking forward to this evening. He came back with a bottle of Pinot Grigio in an ice bucket for the girls and two pints of Bud for the boys. They all ordered steak, and they all liked it medium rare, with veg, chips, tobacco onions, creamed potatoes, and peppered sauce. The bar was quiet enough, and it wasn't long before they took over, filling the bar with their laughter and fun. Their dinner was delicious, and they sat on chatting and drinking until Johnny asked Mal if he fancied a game of pool.

'More wine before you go please,' Nicole said, shaking her wine glass at Johnny. Of course, Johnny obliged, kissing Nicole before he went and as he returned. The boys played pool, while the girls sat at a table nearby them, and it reminded Sally of the night Mal had arrived; she was in the pub in Culdaff dining alone, people-watching. The young girls had been watching their boyfriends play pool; little did she know then the difference a few days would make – that she would be sitting with Nicole, watching Mal and Johnny play that same game. Watching Mal was a joy in itself, as he stretched over the table, his shoulders and arms straining the material of that perfect white shirt, his taut, very sexy bum all groppable in those jeans. She walked past on the way to the ladies and did what she'd been wanting to do; she squeezed his ass as he bent to take a shot. The cue jolted forward as did he; he hit the white but nothing else.

'Two shots!' Johnny announced.

She made an attempt to keep walking, but he caught her by the waist with one arm and lifted her off the ground; she was just above him, his other hand still holding the cue. He said, 'You will pay for that, madam.'

'If you lose now, then revenge *will be sweet*,' she sang the last three words with one eyebrow lifted but holding his stare. He remembered her words from the beach, and he howled, laughing. He set her to her feet, kissed her deeply, and smacked her ass. 'If you don't stop smacking my ass, I won't know whether I've taken these red jeans off or not in the morning.'

'Never, babe,' he said, swigging his beer. Johnny won the game by the time she came back from the ladies . . .

They had a few more drinks before asking the barman to ring them a taxi. Opening another bottle of wine was the last thing the girls needed, but when Johnny asked the time back in the mobile, the girls sang in chorus, 'Wine time', and fell back on the sofa, hugging each other and enjoying the craic with themselves. The boys would have needed another case of beer in them to catch up on their drunken states, but the craic was good, and they were all enjoying each other's company. The girls had one more glass of wine and K.O.-ed on the sofa, Sally's head on Mal's lap and Nicole's head on Sally's. Johnny took a picture on his phone to slag them in the morn. Then he lifted Nicole to bed. Mal tucked Sally in too, and the boys had another beer. Mal asked questions about Johnny and Nicole's relationship, realising he didn't know much about them as a couple. Johnny told Mal what he had expected and that he was crazy in love with Nicole. He let Mal in on his secret. He hadn't told a soul that he'd bought a ring to propose to Nicole.

'When Jim and Anna get back from Sligo, I am going to ask for their blessing,' Johnny said proudly. Mal congratulated him, saying it'd taken him long enough.

'Hey, man, we could make it a double proposal,' Mal added, taking a drink of beer and looking at Johnny for his reaction.

'Seriously? Jaysus, you're only back.'

Mal shook his head. 'Am never letting her out of my sight again, man, and judging by those two', Mal nodded towards the bedrooms, 'they come as a twosome, sooo, so should we?'

'Brilliant,' exclaimed Johnny, 'let's do it, mate.' The boys stood, then man-hugged to seal the deal. They spent an hour or more bouncing ideas off each other about their upcoming proposals. When they came to an idea, they both got excited, and there was another man hug and clink of beers . . .

Chapter 13

Nicole and Johnny left Culdaff to go home on Thursday. They both had the rest of the week off, but they wanted to give Sally and Mal some alone time. Sally knew she would miss them but was looking forward to being alone again with Mal.

They stayed in Culdaff until Sunday morning, their days spent between bed and the beach. On Saturday night, they walked to the beach at midnight. They found themselves a rocky surround and made love on the sand with the sound of the white horses crashing, as the tide made its way along the sandy shore towards them. It was the perfect last night in Culdaff on their own, getting to know one another again and again. The next day, they were going back to Derry, and Mal would gatecrash 'Elizabeth, John, and Sally's time'. Sunday dinner would be the four of them and hopefully stay that way. She couldn't wait to reintroduce Mal to her parents. They had always been fond of him, and she knew they would be again. They locked up the mobile home and drove their own cars back. Mal had booked into a bed and breakfast when he first got back and was paid up for two weeks, but Sally wasn't having it. So he went and collected the rest of his things and thanked the lady who owned the house. The lady was delighted getting two weeks' money for nothing and gave Mal her card to 'come back any time'.

Back at Sally's apartment, they unpacked, with Sally clearing one drawer in the bedroom and one in the bathroom for Mal's bits and pieces. Mal casually dropped in that he would make them a whole new bedroom set for their new house when he got his business up and running. Sally was rendered speechless. Everything was happening so fast; it wasn't a complaint, but it did give her a head rush. When she didn't say anything, Mal took her in his arms from behind, kissing her neck, and said, 'If am rushing you or getting any of this wrong, promise me you will tell me, Sal. I am bound to make mistakes. This is all new to me but everything I have ever wanted, so I can't afford to mess things up.'

She turned in his arms to face him so she could look into his eyes to say, 'You're not rushing me. I just can't believe this is all happening. It is way too amazing, and I keep waiting for the "boom" back to earth again.'

'This is it, baby,' he replied. 'Get used to it because we have waited way too long for it,' he said, swatting her backside. 'Now let's go have dinner at your parents'.' Sally had texted her mum that morning as soon as she got a signal on her phone.

Leaving Culdaff today. Guess who's coming to dinner?

It was her nana's favourite film, starring Sidney Poitier, Katherine Hepburn, and Spencer Tracy. She knew her mum would get the double sentiment.

Can't wait to hear all x

Was the text she received straight back. She had a feeling Nicole or Anna had already been in touch with her mum.

Chapter 14

Sally was nervous going in through the front door of her parents' house, but if Mal was, he didn't show it. Hugs, kisses, and handshaking greeted them at the door. Elizabeth and John straight away offered their condolences for Mal's mum. Mal had already told John the story of his mum not sending the letters, so there was no need to go over it again; this was the last hurdle – getting Sally's mum and dad to trust him again.

Over dinner of roast beef with all the trimmings, they spoke of their Easter breaks and the fun both couples had. Sally and Mal loaded the dishwasher while her mum and dad relaxed in the garden.

'That went well,' said Mal. 'I thought they might have still hated me.'

'They never hated you, Mal. I don't think they ever could.' They joined her parents in the garden and enjoyed the rest of their relaxing Sunday evening together.

Mal had arranged to meet John for lunch at his office the next day. When he got there, Elizabeth was sitting on the end of his desk, legs dangling like a schoolgirl. Dressed in black capri pants and a camel waist-length cape, she looked very elegant, every bit the blonde Liz Hurley. Knowing John was a 'straight to the point' man much like himself, Mal came straight out with it.

'I want to marry her, John.'

Elizabeth nearly fell off the desk (more like Liz MacDonald on the booze in The Rovers.)

'I love her so much, always have. I can't ever be without her again.'

John, who was not easily stunned, was lost for words.

'Mal, you're only back, son. This is so sudden,' Elizabeth shrieked.

John never took his eyes off Mal the whole time; Mal could feel them burning into him as if he was trying to get inside his head. He eventually spoke, stroking his jaw with his thumb and forefinger, 'Elizabeth, you know Sally better than anyone. Do you think she would say yes? And most of all, do you think she would have the happily ever after she deserves?'

Elizabeth took a deep breath, then stood and settled on the edge of her husband's plush desk chair and answered, 'Yes, yes, I believe she would, on both accounts.' John stood, taking Elizabeth with him. He put his left arm around her waist and extended his other hand out to Mal.

'Good luck, son. Don't let her down.'

Mal went ring shopping as soon as he left John and a very excited Elizabeth.

He texted Johnny:

> *all systems go man. Just got the thumbs up.*

> *Serious? Great! I better get a move on then lol. I will chat to them tonight.*

Mal texted him right back with a wide grin on his face.

> *lol good luck man*

Tuesday was a beautiful day again. Sally and Mal went into the town. Mal said he had a surprise for her. They went to Johnny's workplace, she assumed to say hello. Johnny had brochures spread out on his table, a big smile on his face.

'What's all this?' asked Sally, looking from Mal to Johnny, totally confused.

'Take your pick, baby.'

The houses on the brochures were stunning and very expensive. Johnny announced he had made appointments to view them all within the next week, starting right now. 'Sea Mist' was the name of the first house. It was built five years ago, with a grey slate facing on the exterior of the house – five bedrooms, three en-suites, and a huge kitchen with rich cream high-gloss cabinets and a black granite worktop. It was simply stunning in the brochure, and Sally, even without seeing the house for herself, fell in love with the name and the kitchen. When they went to see it, it just confirmed its own beauty. The drive had perfectly manicured lawns on both sides. The sun shone to the left side where a conservatory sat shining, surrounded in bright flowers. The patio was built up with plant pots filled with beautiful, colourful flowers (which would have to be passed by Nicole's *The Language of Flowers*); it was breath-taking and she hadn't even got inside yet.

'Mal, can we afford the mortgage for this?' she asked, getting out of the car in a state of shock mixed with surprise and excitement.

'Baby, I forgot to tell you. Am minted,' he laughed. 'We will be buying it with cash.'

Sally's mouth hit her chest. 'Oh my God, how? Jeez, I can't believe all this, Mal.' She turned and looked back at the house. 'It is soo beautiful!'

'Shall I ring Johnny and tell him we'll take it?'

She was about to say that they hadn't been inside yet but stopped. It didn't matter; she had seen the kitchen and the surrounding gardens, and that was enough to go by to know the rest of the house would be equally as stunning. She got a lovely homey feeling that you didn't get just anywhere, and with Mal back in her life, she couldn't imagine a more beautiful home for them to start the rest of their life together. 'Yes, yes, please, oh, thank you.' She jumped up into his arms and wrapped her legs around his waist.

'My grandparents owned a lot of land, Sal. I sold it for a hell of a lot of money. It was prime building land in Madrid and I had, at one stage, eight builders bidding for it. We will be comfortable, babes, and, most of all, happy.' *kiss* He slapped her bum that he still had in his hands, with her legs still wrapped around him, and kissed her again.

They called at her mum and dad's that evening with the brochure of Sea Mist. Her mum was so excited and she also loved the name and kitchen; she couldn't wait to get the guided tour of the whole house. Sally told her about the garden and patio and how magical it looked.

'A dream home,' her mum sang.

'I feel like I'm in a dream most of the time,' Sally replied. All four of them left to go out to dinner to celebrate.

Sally was exhausted by the time she got home to the apartment, and they went straight to bed with lots of thoughts of grey slate, flowers, and beautiful kitchen.

Mal met up with Johnny the next day to look at properties for his new business. He certainly was not letting the grass grow under his feet. They looked at a few, and Mal was indecisive over two. He left Johnny to go pick Sally up to take her to see them with him again. His mind was on overdrive. His dreams were all falling into place: Sally, the dream house, and now his business would be up and running soon. He had a permanent smile on his face. He knew it and loved it. The very thought of making Sally happy made him very, very happy indeed. His life was changing so quickly and all for the better; he couldn't believe how lucky he was. The contentment he had ached for the last ten years was finally settling in. Nothing or no one could take it from him or dampen his mood . . .

He didn't see the white van until it was too late . . .

Sally was cleaning and tidying when she got a text from Mal.

It's a toss-up between 2. I will pick u up in half hour to go c them x

She texted him back.

K babes c u soon xx

Chapter 15

*A*n hour had passed and still no sign of him, so she rang him, but no answer. She rang Johnny, thinking he had got caught up with him talking business. Johnny told her he had left him about an hour ago. She waited and waited but still no sign or reply to her text. Her stomach was in turmoil by now, and she was wearing a pathway on the living room carpet, pacing up and down with the phone in her right hand and the finger of her left in and out of her mouth, biting down on it out of sheer panic. Going into the fourth hour, her anxiety was through the roof. She had called her dad, but he hadn't heard from him; she rang Nicole, in case Johnny had heard anything, but nothing. Nicole and Johnny came straight over after stopping at both the new units first to check for him there. Nicole kept boiling the kettle as if to make coffee but never got round to making a cup; it was just a distraction. Johnny kept trying Mal's mobile number, but nothing. He phoned the solicitor to ask if he had heard from him, but he hadn't. They were running out of options. At this stage, Sally had stopped pacing and just curled up on her cuddle chair with her phone on the arm, her head thumping and heavy with thoughts. Nicole and Johnny were chatting in the kitchen. Sally could hear their voices, but she was so distracted she couldn't hear what they were saying. When Nicole suggested phoning the hospital, Sally nearly vomited; she was torn between thinking he'd left her again and that he'd been hurt badly. Neither option was sufferable. Nicole did the work; she got the number of Altnagelvin Hospital's A&E Department and rang them, asking if there was a Malacey Quinn admitted at any time that day. Sally listened to her own heartbeat pounding in her ears and tried to hear the conversation Nicole was having, but she could see from Nicole's face it was bad news; before Nicole hung up the phone, she had tears threatening to fall from her eyes.

'No, no, no,' she kept repeating as Nicole told her, 'He's been admitted, Sally. That's all they can tell me on the phone. We need to get over there.'

Johnny, Nicole, and Sally were in Johnny's car within seconds. Johnny sped over the bridge and up the link, and they were at the hospital within fifteen minutes. They waited twenty agonising minutes for a doctor to come and talk to them. Dr Loftus led them to a room and introduced herself, explaining that Mal was in a road traffic accident. A transit van had hit him head-on, and he had head injuries. She said Mal was in the theatre still, and the surgeon would let them know how it had gone.

'The man in the van wasn't so lucky,' said Dr Loftus. 'He wasn't wearing a seat belt and was thrown from the van. He died instantly.'

Sally felt weak, and Nicole attempted to wrap her arms around her, but she had to run. She was going to be sick and she could only make it to the bin at the door. The realisation of what had just happened and just how serious it all was, was settling in. She couldn't wait to see him, to wrap her arms around him. She couldn't imagine not being able to. And how would he be? Would he be brain damaged for the rest of his life? Would he recognise her? Would he be the same Mal? There were no answers. Not yet anyway. It was just a waiting game. Nicole had rung Sally's parents to tell them. Elizabeth and John came right away, and John scooped Sally up into his arms. John sat with her in his lap and Elizabeth next to them, Sally's head resting back on her dad's chest. Sally was silent, feeling numb inside. She couldn't allow herself to think because the thoughts were disturbing; they were all negative, and she couldn't face them. The clock ticked above the blue door of the waiting room, but time was dragging. No one knew what to say, so most of the time was spent in silence. Nicole and Johnny went to get coffee for everyone, just for something to do. While they were gone, the surgeon arrived. He had bags under his eyes; he looked overworked and tired.

Sally jumped up. 'Please tell me he's going to be OK,' she croaked; her throat was dry and her voice scratched it.

The surgeon introduced himself as Mr Houston. He was emotionless and his tone unwavering. 'Mr Quinn has just had four hours of surgery.

At the minute, he is stable, but the next forty-eight hours are crucial. He had swelling of the brain. We drilled a hole in the skull to relieve the swelling, and we have him in a medically induced coma at the minute until the swelling goes down. Time will tell if his injury is permanent or if he will need more surgery. Am sorry, that's all I can tell you for now.'

Sally was weak and speechless.

'Can we see him?' whispered Elizabeth.

'Yes, I will have the nurse show you to his room.' With that, Mr Houston was gone. Two minutes later, the nurse came through the door with a sympathetic smile and motioned to the door, her arms stretched as if to say, 'After you' although she left first, maybe to give them time to gather themselves.

She led them to a corridor that looked short but seemed to go on forever. When they got to the door of Mal's room, Sally could see him through the little rectangle window on the door; her stomach churned. Walking through the door took all the strength she could gather up. There were tubes, leads, sticky discs on his chest, and the beep, beep, beep of the monitors; she couldn't focus on any of that. All she could see was Mal lying there helpless, and there was nothing she could do to help him. She felt helpless too. Her mum, dad, Nicole, and Johnny left Sally alone with Mal after about fifteen minutes. She sat beside him, not knowing whether to touch him, talk to him, or just wrap her arms around him in any way possible. She fought the urge to climb into the bed beside him, pull the blankets up over their heads, and block out reality. But she couldn't; she just sat staring at him, not even crying, just staring at this beautiful, handsome, helpless man that she loved and had just got a second chance with, and now she could lose him again and forever this time . . .

She laid her arms on the bed and rested her head on them, looking towards his face; her eyes got heavy after an hour and a half of just sitting there staring, going between resting her head on her arms that rested on the bed and stretching the top half of her body out. The next she felt was her mum's hand on her shoulder, waking her. She was disorientated at first, then realisation kicked in, and she burst into tears; her mum just held her in her arms as tight as she could, trying to silently reassure her but failing miserably. The only reassurance she needed was for Mal to wake up and take her in his arms and never let go. Elizabeth broke the silence when Sally's cries became sobs and sniffles.

'It's half past one in the morning, darling. Do you want to go home with us and come back first thing in the morning?'

'No, Mum, I can't leave him. You all go. I have to stay.'

'OK, OK, do you want me to stay with you, darling?' asked Elizabeth, stroking her daughter's hair.

'No, you go, but can you bring my toothbrush and bits and bobs in the morning, please?' sniffed Sally.

'Of course, darling, text if you can think of anything else.' Kissing her daughter on the forehead, Elizabeth left reluctantly.

After another half an hour of staring at Mal blankly, Sally fell in and out of sleep, waking ever so often with a banging headache and the buzzing and beeping of monitors. At half past six in the morning, the nurse came in and introduced herself as Amanda; she was in her mid-fifties, with jet-black hair and eyebrows pencilled in the same darkness of her hair. She checked Mal's monitors and wrote her findings on the chart at the bottom of his bed. She was quiet but still had a caring, approachable air about her. Sally just watched her do her thing, not knowing what to ask or if she even wanted to hear the possible answers. 'He's doing well, dear,' she said in a raspy voice. Sally just nodded. 'Talk to him, tell him how much you miss him,' said Amanda, nodding at Mal.

'I feel mute,' admitted Sally. 'I just can't get any words out. I don't know what to say to him.'

'That's common, my dear. It will come to you. Would you like a paper to try reading to him, first of all?' Nurse Amanda offered, but Sally just shook her head, dismissing the idea of reading a newspaper to him, like you might to an old man you would visit in an old person's home, out of pity. She felt angry at the thought, the thought that someone could suggest this – to read a newspaper to Mal; he was so independent and strong. She refused to think this was going to be her only way of communicating with him. She felt like shaking him awake, like screaming at him, 'Get up, get up.' Her blood was boiling over. Her body felt like it was about to combust; her throat was closing over, and she felt like she was in the octagon and Conor Mc Gregor had her by the throat. She had to get out of the room. She had to take a minute, so she went to the bathroom while the nurse was still with him. She locked the door and grabbed her hair with both hands, her eyes closed tight, but the tears still escaped; she was going to explode. She couldn't catch a breath, and it was strangling her. After falling to the ground on to her bum and stamping her feet as hard as she could, her body shaking with emotion and anger and fear, she curled herself into a ball, cuddling herself and sobbing into her arms. She didn't know how long she lay there on the cold hard floor, thinking of how hard done by she was, how unfair life was, and how much her life was going to change. She had herself nearly convinced that these were the cards she had been dealt with. She was a great believer in fate and always said, 'What will be, will be.' So she was trying to accept that Mal was returned to her just so she could look after him – so she could feed him and wash him and . . . and . . . A rattle at the door pulled her out of her self-pity. Slowly she got to her feet, avoiding the mirror over the sink, and threw cold water over her face, drying it with a hard, scratchy paper hand towel. She took deep breaths and opened the door to go back to a room where lay the love of her life, slowly leaving her *again* . . .

Back in Mal's room, Amanda was still there; she took one look at Sally and asked her if her family were on their way over to her. Sally shrugged her shoulders and fell into silence again. Amanda touched her shoulder and left the room. At 9.30 a.m. Elizabeth's head popped around the door, searching for Sally, and John followed shortly after her with the daily paper and a holdall containing toiletries and a change of clothes for Sally. She thanked them, and they sat in silence for a half an hour before two doctors came through the doors, introducing themselves as doctor this and that and the other. She couldn't focus; she just wanted to hear about Mal and how he was going to make a complete recovery, not *their* names and ranks. They looked in his eyes, checked his notes, and were gone again. The next few days were much the same. Mal looked the same; the beep, beep, beeping sound was the same, and Sally's heart and emotions were all the same too. Only the nurses changed, but it was mostly Amanda that came in, and Sally was really warming to her, even knowing she hadn't taken the time to speak to her much, but she was always very caring to both Sally and Mal. Elizabeth and John arrived every morning to sit with their daughter but felt as helpless as she did. Doctors came and went, and unless they told Sally Mal was going to wake up in five minutes, she didn't want to hear much of what they said, not that they spoke much. On the fourth day, the same two doctors that came in on the first morning entered Mal's room. 'He's responding well,' one doctor said. 'He is a big strong lad and has fight in him,' he finished with an empty smile; the other doctor just looked at the chart at the end of Mal's bed and waited for his colleague to stop with his bedside mannerisms, clearly not having any himself. She sat and watched again in silence, but with a very heavy heart. Once again, no question was worth the chance of an answer she couldn't handle. The doctor hadn't told her anything she didn't already know. Mal *was* a big strong lad. Mal *had* fight in him. But right now, he was lying helpless in a hospital bed, and no one could promise her he would return to her as the Mal she knew and loved. The doctors left without another word, John at their heels.

'Darling, why don't you go and get cleaned up, and I will sit with him?' Elizabeth said, pulling Sally out of her daze.

Sally stood at the mirror in the bathroom of the hospital; this time she decided she could face the reflection that would look back at her. After she washed her face and brushed her teeth and hair, pulling it back into a low ponytail, she looked at her tired washed-out face with black rings under her eyes and a taut mouth. She looked aged and worn out. Taking a heavy breath in and out, she looked into the mirror and into her own eyes; she squinted at herself with an industrious thought and decided there and then she was going to think positive; she was going to give herself a shake and go and chat to Mal, try and talk him round, so to speak. With a new-found determination, she took a deep breath in and out a few times and unlocked the door. As she left, she saw her dad talking to one of the doctors that had just left Mal's room. She paused for a moment to read the expression on her dad's face; for a split second, she thought of turning and locking herself in the bathroom again, but when she saw her dad smiling and nodding, looking positive and maybe a bit relieved, she felt a surge of hope run through her veins and push her on towards Mal's room. She watched her dad enter first, and she followed him in a matter of seconds. It was clear he was starting to fill her mum in. 'Good, I can tell you both at the same time,' said John with a smile, holding his arm out for his daughter to walk into. 'Mal's doing good, pet. The doctors are very hopeful he will make a good recovery. It won't be today or tomorrow. He's in for a time of it, but he's strong and young, and his signs are improving every day.' John's positive words made her cry again, with a little surge of relief this time.

Chapter 16

The following few days, Sally sat at Mal's side, chatting about their past and their future in their new home. She bought lots of magazines and flicked through the 'home' ones and told him of her plans she had for each room in the house, speaking of ideas and colour schemes and the plans she had for BBQs in the summer and overnight visits from Nicole and Johnny for dinner and drinks in the winter evenings. 'I will have to get you to make a plaque with "Nicole and Johnny's room" on it,' she said and then explained that little thought. She read him the headlines of the newspapers (only the gossip and interesting ones, no boring or horror stories). Nicole called on Sally at the hospital every day with lunch for her and Sally; most days, it was all she ate. On the tenth day, the doctors decided to bring Mal slowly out of his coma; by the twelfth day, Mal's eyes started to flicker, but nothing much else. On the thirteenth day, Mal opened his eyes for a short while; they were glazy and unfocused, but Sally was so excited to be finally able to look into his big brown eyes that it took her about thirty seconds before she thought to call the nurse. It was Nurse Amanda that came after she pressed the buzzer. 'Hello, handsome,' Amanda said, standing over Mal, looking down into his eyes with a light while lifting his eyelids.

Sally felt both a pang of jealousy and a rush of pride run through her at the nurse's words, but then the excitement of Mal waking up was too overwhelming, and she found herself panicking again. 'Will he be OK? Is this normal? Can he see me, hear me?' She knew she was asking too many questions at once, but she couldn't help herself.

'It's all good signs, my dear. Keep chatting to him, but keep it light. Don't ask questions of him. Don't ask him about the accident either. He will remember that in his own time. Just reassure him you're here for him.' Nurse Amanda rubbed Sally's shoulders with a reassuring hand. 'You are doing good too, my dear.' And off she went and left Sally to start her one-sided conversation again. After a few hours, Sally's throat was dry from chatting and reading; she knew she was chatting about silly stuff like where she would like them both to holiday next or eat out next, about dresses she had seen in some of the magazines she looked through, and as she looked for a topic to speak of, Nicole's garden came up in her one-sided conversation. She tried to remember the flowers and their meanings; she was sure she had got them all wrong. Her both hands were holding Mal's right hand. 'I love you so much, babes,' she started to repeat over and over and then, as if he was answering her, he squeezed her hand lightly, but it was still something – hope, and that was exactly what she needed. She kept chatting, laughing, and crying all at once; she felt, for the first time in an age, her heartbeat strong in her ribcage. Sally held on to his hand for all she was worth, for everything they were worth together and hoping for more. She wasn't disappointed; very softly, he tightened his fingers in hers. Sally pushed the buzzer for a nurse, wanting to share the good news. She texted Nicole and her mum with one hand, not daring to let go of Mal's with the other. The messages she got back were all shared excitement. Sally just covered Mal's face in tiny swift kisses. 'Please wake up, Mal. Please, babes, please wake up.' She was on repeat until a nurse came in and needed the space she was sharing with Mal. Sally reluctantly stepped back, keeping hold of his hand in hers, and he flexed again, tighter this time, and Sally let out a shocked, relieved giggle. 'He did it again, look, look.' His fingers were still slightly wiggling, and his eyes flickered at the same time. They were still unfocused, rolling around in his head; it was scary looking at them, but she knew it was all good signs nonetheless.

The nurse did her checks, noted her findings, and told Sally she would inform the consultant, but before she left, she said, 'Looks like he's pretty determined to get back to you.' And with a big smile she left. Sally couldn't help a big smile too.

Nicole and Johnny had been on their way when they received the text. Nicole hugged Sally with both arms, but Sally only hugged back with one as she kept hold of Mal's with the other. Nicole leant over Mal, saying, 'Jaysus, Mal, would you hurry up and get outta that bed? I need my bestie back.' Both girls laughed; the sound was foreign, but very welcome.

Chapter 17

*O*ver the next few days, Mal's eyes opened for longer and longer periods every time, and Sally could tell he was recognising her and she even had seen a small smile on his beautiful face. She never left his side, only to wash and pee. Elizabeth and John, Nicole and Johnny, and even Anna came to visit, but she never took their offer of sitting with him; while she got fresh air, she didn't want to miss a beat. He went from eyes flickering and unfocused to chatting for a minute, but he would get tired quickly. He was making a good recovery, and they could start to see a light at the end of that long, long tunnel that had been hanging around like a bad smell. Five and a half weeks and lots of tests and physiotherapy later, he was allowed to come home with a warning of taking things easy. Mr Houston, the surgeon, came in to do a quick check before Mal was discharged. He warned Mal to take things slowly and listen to his own body and rest if needed. He also informed him how lucky he was and told him not everyone made such a full recovery, but he had high expectations of Mal doing just that.

'I had to get back to my girl, Doc,' said Mal, his eyes burning into Sally's face, taking in everything about her, her weight loss and the black bags under her eyes. He *had* to get better, and although he didn't do this on purpose, he hated that he was the cause of the agonised expression written all over her otherwise flawless face. Before they left Mal's room, he put an arm around her waist, looked into her tired eyes, and said, 'Am gonna make your eyes smile again soon, baby.' kiss

Sally's parents collected them both from the hospital and left them off at Sally's apartment, where Nicole and Johnny had balloons and banners and champagne ready for them. Mal was tired but grateful, and he was even more grateful when they left a half an hour and one glass of bubbly later.

'Home and alone at last,' Mal said, as Sally flopped on to the sofa next to him after leaving Nicole and Johnny at the door, kissing them both and thanking them from the bottom of her heart for everything they had done for her. Everyone had felt helpless while Mal was in his coma; no one knew what the outcome was to be, but she just knew she had Nicole and Johnny as well as her mum and dad for continued support for as long as she needed them, and it was a great blanket for her.

She laid her head on his shoulder now and rubbed his chest. 'Am so happy to have you back home. I was so scared, Mal.'

'Shh,' said Mal, pushing her hair back from her face. He could hear her voice breaking. 'Please promise me you will look after yourself, Sal. You have lost way too much weight.' Mal kissed her hand as he held it, then added, 'Now go phone for some Chinese takeaway, and let's get you fattened up a bit.' Sally playfully slapped him on the arm and went for her phone.

Sally fussed about getting him into bed. She fluffed his pillows and tucked him in like you would a toddler. Mal got tired very soon after they ate their Chinese food. He was tired, which was to be expected for the next few weeks, maybe months. He fell asleep quite quickly in her bed, and Sally took the time to relax in a bubble bath. She used to bathe every night when she was on her own. She preferred a bath to a shower. She missed relaxing and feeling the bubbles popping around her. She lay back, and for the first time in five and a half weeks, she relaxed. She lay in the bath for an hour, topping it up with hot water now and again. She de-fuzzed, body-buttered herself from head to toe, dried her hair, and instantly felt more like herself. She checked in on Mal every few minutes, checking his breathing if he was too quiet, just like a new mum would check her newborn baby. She crawled across the bed and lay beside him, stroking his stubble on his olive cheeks. She didn't think she could sleep, but she woke two hours later to find Mal stroking her hair back from her face.

'I love your eyes,' he whispered, letting her wake up slowly.

'Mal,' she cried, tears falling fresh and fast, surprising herself as well as Mal.

'Hey, hey, what's up, baby?'

'I . . . I don't know. It's just I . . . I think am just so relieved to have you home,' she blubbered. He stroked her hair more, kissing her forehead and whispering loving, reassuring words in her ears as he nibbled them too. She fell fast asleep again, and when she woke, he wasn't in bed. He was on the phone, and she followed his voice to the kitchen.

'See you soon, man.' He hung up as she entered.

'Nic and Johnny are bringing breakfast. Am starving and there's nothing in the fridge, woman.' He stood with his two arms flung out, his phone still in one of them.

'Aye, sorry about that. I guess I forgot while I was swarming around the town, pampering myself and shoppi—'

He cut her off by covering her mouth with his in a big, wet, sloppy kiss. 'Thanks for looking after me in there.' He was serious now.

'You're welcome, but don't go doing anything like that again soon . . . or try *ever*, Mal Quinn.' She swatted his shoulder and he winced. 'Ooh, sorry, babes, sorry, sorry, did I . . . ?' He laughed, and she swatted him harder.

'Seriously, Sal, thank you, babes. I know you never left my side, and I won't ever forget that.'

'How did you know? Could you hear me, feel me?'

'Naw, I smelt you. Were you not allowed to use the showers in there or what?' She could have thumped him again, but she was so glad he was back to his teasing self and she just feigned embarrassment and shock. He grabbed her by the waist and spun them both in a half circle. 'You smell good enough to eat right now though.' *kiss*

'What a corny line, Mal Quinn!' *kiss*

Johnny brought paperwork over as well as breakfast. They all ate at the kitchen table, and the boys stayed there with the paperwork, while the girls tidied and went for a roll on their boots. Sally was glad to get out for a bit of exercise, and when Nicole suggested going up the quay on their roller boots, Sally jumped at the chance; she also felt it was pre-planned between Nicole and Johnny.

'All systems go with the house and just a few fine details on the business unit to finalise,' Johnny said proudly; he had even got Mal a solicitor to make a house call. 'It is nearly unheard of, smug assholes,' Johnny said. 'But this guy's dead on,' Johnny assured. Mal trusted Johnny to know his stuff, and the deals were going ahead as planned.

It would be a while before Mal could get started on his business side of things; he knew he wasn't totally back to himself yet. He got tired very easily, but every day, he was determined to get stronger, physically and mentally. Mal really wanted Johnny to push the house as fast as he could. He couldn't wait to see Sal in that house, her face beaming with pride and his beaming back at her. He felt stronger every day and thanked the Lord for his health, but every day, he said a wee prayer for the poor guy in the white transit van that didn't make it. They didn't speak much about the accident, but the white van and the man's face was the last he remembered until he came around and saw Sal's blurred face in the hospital.

The car he had been driving at the time of the accident was a rental, and he didn't give a shit about it. But now, he really needed to buy his own car. His six-foot-four-inch frame getting out of Sal's wee red beetle was a comical sight. It was hard enough work getting into the bloody thing without worrying about getting out again. With his laptop on the kitchen table, he typed in 'auto trader'. A few phone calls later, Johnny and Mal were making the hour and ten minutes journey to a garage in Toome to look at a 5 series.

Sally's boss rang her, asking about Mal. 'Is he even your boyfriend, Sally?' she asked in the most condescending tone. 'It's just I didn't know you even had one.'

'Bitch.' Sally covered the mouthpiece of the phone, then answered, 'Yes, Victoria, he's my boyfriend, and I will be back at work next week.' She clicked off before she told her boss to shove her job somewhere uncomfortable and just as she heard her shout, 'Next week?'

She was still fuming by the time she checked the text she'd heard beep while she was in the bathroom on the home phone to stuck-up Vic.

Come downstairs to the parking area, beside ur beetle x

Shit whts up babe? coming xx

The first thing to run through her mind was her beetle was hit and damaged, but Mal had the biggest smile on his face as he saw her at the end of the stairs and look through the double glass doors towards the parking area. Sally's mouth dropped open. 'Ohh, Mal, it's beautiful.' His grinning proud face was infectious, and she felt just as proud of him. It was the brightest white BMW with deep red leather upholstery. The windows had dark tint, and the dashboard was like a cockpit, lit up and so many dials and buttons to adjust this and that. It definitely suited a big hunk of a man like Mal Quinn. 'You boys and your toys,' Sally said, laughing when Johnny said, like a baby coveting another baby's toy, 'I want one!' That night they went out for dinner; Mal drove for an hour and ten minutes to a restaurant he had passed in Toome, where he bought the car; he thought it *looked* nice. Sally smiled, knowing full well it was an excuse to drive his hot new wheels. The meal was lovely but not worth the petrol getting there. There were lots of beautiful restaurants to eat at in Derry. Sally could have named at least ten she would have loved to eat at. After dinner, Sally could see the day had taken its toll on Mal; he was tired and asked Sally to drive home. Of course, Sally was delighted to drive the BMW. Mal got himself comfortable and slept the whole way home.

Chapter 18

In and out of furniture shops was not as much fun as Sally thought it would be, and she was conscious that Mal would tire easily, so after Sally fell in love with a beautiful 3+2+1 sofa selection in silver grey and black, she decided she would go for purple accessories, which she would buy online, and home they went with lunch in a bag from Centra's Deli counter. Sally's phone beeped with a new message, and when she read it, she wasn't sure how to answer it. Mal saw her face and asked, 'What's up, babes?'

'Mum just texted, saying it's girls' night at hers.'

'And?'

'Well, I don't want to leave you on your own yet,' she answered with a shrug of her shoulders.

'Aww, baby, you haven't had a night to yourself since I turned up again. Go get drunk with the girls and enjoy yourself.' Then he added, 'As much as you can without me, of course.' kiss 'You are back to work next week. You might as well enjoy.' *kiss*

'We used to do this every Wednesday night without fail.'

Mal's brows pulled together. 'Ohh, I don't think I could spare you every Wednesday, so go enjoy tonight.' Sally wasn't sure if he was joking or not, but when he smacked her bum and told her he was, she was relieved; she didn't know what she would do if Mal started to tell her what she could and couldn't do. Another text came through; this time it was on Mal's phone. 'It's Johnny,' said Mal. 'Three guesses what he's been told to do.'

So Sally left Johnny and Mal with a box of beer and paperwork and plans spread across the coffee table. Nicole and Johnny came over in a taxi, and Nicole was waiting in it for Sally. They left to go and pick Anna up too. Elizabeth had left out all the nibbles on the table and the wine glasses were polished to within an inch of their life. John was in the living room reading, while the girls sat at the kitchen island, chatting and catching up on a few weeks' gossip. Sally stopped near her dad first, to kiss him hello before making her way to the kitchen too. Everyone agreed Sally had lost way too much weight while Mal was ill, and her mum told her she should look after herself or she would move them both in with her and look after them both herself. Sally loved her mum and dad to bits but couldn't handle the thought of living under their roof again and definitely not with Mal too. So she promised to get back to normal as soon as possible.

'Speaking of moving in, when do you get your keys for your new house?' Anna asked.

'Two weeks' time, I think.'

'And what are you planning on doing with your apartment, Sally? Betty Mc Carron's daughter is looking for something just like yours to rent. If you're interested, I can give her your number.'

'Jeez, I haven't even thought about it, but yes, that sounds good. I will let you know, Anna, thanks.'

The more wine and nibbles they had, the more Sally realised how much she had missed this, their little haven of mother–daughter friendship.

John had a late start on Thursday morning, so he offered to run the girls home. When he took the long way by leaving Anna off first, then Nicole, Sally knew he had something on his mind. Sitting in the front of the A4, with her dad driving, she started to feel a little anxious. What is he going to talk to me about? Is it bad news? Does he know something about Mal's injuries that I don't? Everything was running through her mind. Then he pulled up outside her apartment and turned off the engine, turning his body to face her.

'You're happy, pet?' He looked expectantly at her, his eyebrows raised in question.

'Yes, Daddy, I really am,' she said with a mixture of a beaming smile and relief.

'OK, that's good enough for me. I just thought with the accident and everything moving so fast with the house that it might be a bit too much for you. Mal's pretty determined to have you and make you happy, and I wish you both all the luck of the angels, pet.'

Sally wasn't sure, but her big strong daddy could just have got a tiny bit choked up. 'Aww, Daddy.' She threw her arms around his neck and bear-hugged him, and she got a big grizzly bear hug right back.

'Send Johnny down, and I will take him home while am here, pet,' John coughed out.

'OK, night, Daddy, love you.' And away she bounced back to her apartment to wrap her arms around Mal and cuddle him till late morning.

Chapter 19

'We booked a hotel breakaway for the four of us,' Mal said to Sally the following morning, as he strolled from the bedroom to the kitchen, bare-chested, to make her coffee.

'Well, that's a lovely surprise. Where are we off to?'

'Jackson's Hotel in Ballybofey, for next Friday and Saturday night. Then we get the keys of the house that Tuesday.'

Sally was starting to act like Nicole now about her house, all dreamy and excited. 'That's great timing, a wee break before the madness of decorating and moving. So thoughtful of you, babes, thank you.' She kissed his bare shoulder as he poured the coffee into a mug. (He was too tall for her to reach past his shoulders without a stretch.)

'That was my thoughts exactly.' He winked at her.

'Did you just wink at me, Mal Quinn?' Sally's voice was shaky with pending giggles.

'That I did, gorgeous,' he replied, winking again and handing over her coffee in her favourite mug. She noted she hadn't even told him it was her favourite mug.

'Oh, I can't wait. I might go shopping for our break away.'

'Yeah, go burn all those wee cotton things you wear and get some nice lacy stuff,' he said, slapping her ass; he was only half joking, and she knew it was a joke with a jag. She never had anyone special enough in her life to want to go and buy nice underwear for. She was going to 'go to town' for the fancy underwear shopping. It had been on top of her list after their reunion in Culdaff, but things got a bit crazy with the accident and all. Now it seemed everything was starting to fall into place again. Underwear was back at the top of that list.

'Wanna come with me?' Sally expected he would jump at the chance, so she gave him her most suggestive look.

'Underwear shopping? Will you be trying them on?'

'No, ye creep,' she said, smirking as she drank her coffee. 'We can go for lunch after though.' She knew that would seal the deal. Mal always thought about his next meal.

'Aye, that's a deal then,' he agreed, slapping her ass again.

Sally picked a small but cute underwear shop she often drove past and admired but never passed the front door. The bell above the door dinged, announcing their arrival, and the shop owner came rushing out from a back room. 'Good morning, there,' she greeted them with a warm smile, if a bit flustered. 'Gimmie a wee shout if you need anything.'

Sally looked around, admiring lots of fancy lingerie and checking out sizes. Mal would wink and nod at the stuff he liked without a thought of who would see him, although the lady was busying herself on the computer at her desk. She picked out some lovely knickers and bra sets and a few lace chemises. When she was in the changing room out back, she asked the lady if she would discreetly wrap up the 'Oh La La Cheri Red Lace Merry Widow and G-string' set she had spied in the more 'racier' section. She was a little embarrassed and nearly didn't ask, but then the shop had lots of other 'sets' that were a lot saucier than the Merry Widow, and the thought of Mal's face emboldened her.

Mal came to the changing room to her as the lady left with an armful of lace and satin. He nipped at her neck with his mouth and snaked his arms around her, resting his palms on her flat tummy, pulling her back towards him. All she wore was her jeans, and they weren't even buttoned up properly. She let her head tilt back into his embrace, feeling the warmth from him, her heart swelling and eyes turning up into the back of her head under their lids. She took a deep breath, feeling Mal pressed against her from behind. She knew she had to pull herself back to the land of the living and kick Mal out of the changing room; she pivoted in his arms, and his hands moulded to her bum cheeks instantly.

'Get out of here before we get too carried away.' She smiled up into his black irises, and in the most flirtatious stance she could pull off, she stepped back against the curtain so he could get the full experience;

then she turned and bent right over in front of him and put on her wedges so she could at least reach his mouth to kiss him.

His eyes took on a lustful hooded look, and he tightened his palms onto her ass again and touched his lips to her temples, saying, 'Your actions are contradicting your words, Sal.' *kiss* 'You are the most incredibly beautiful and sexy sight, baby. But I got to warn you not to look at me like that again, unless you want me to bang you senseless on this spot.'

She swatted his shoulder and went on to her tiptoes to kiss his jaw. 'You're soo romantic, babes.' Rolling her eyes and giggling, she pushed both his shoulders with both her hands and got him out so she could pull herself together and get dressed.

The lovely lady had all her goods wrapped and bagged in beautiful boxes and paper bags with strings and bows, and Mal had everything paid for when she got to the checkout desk. Thanking the lady, off they went, Sally with a glow about her, because she knew she had a surprise Mal would love . . .

After the underwear shopping, Sally fancied a new outfit too, so they walked the stairs in Foyleside Shopping Centre, hand in hand, to River Island. Mal went upstairs to the men's, and Sally stayed downstairs in the ladies, flicking through rails of different items; she was thinking about their weekend away and how lovely it would be when she felt his arms come from behind her and snake around her waist, tugging her back towards his body. She leant her head back on his chest, saying, 'You didn't take long.' She instantly felt it. It was all wrong, and he wasn't the right height; nor did he smell like Mal. The voice in her ear confirmed it.

'Hey, beautiful, I've missed you.'

She turned around in a flash. 'Michael, Jesus, what are you doing?'

'No one makes my coffee as good as you do. Please come back to work soon, beautiful,' he said in a carefree manner, but he still had a hand on her waist when she heard Mal's voice.

'Want to remove your hand from my girl's body, *lad*?!' It wasn't a question, and he had murderous eyes, his tone a definite warning not to be ignored. Mal put his arm around Sally's shoulders, pulling her back to his chest, putting *his* property back into the arms of its rightful owner . . . *him*. His jaw was pulsing due to his teeth grinding. His chest heaving, he was trying his best to hold on to his decorum and not make a show, but his whole body was betraying his intent.

'Hey, no bother, boss.' Michael was clearly intimidated but tried to sound confident. Sally was frightened; Michael's cockiness could earn him a slap in the middle of River Island. He just lifted his hands up in a surrender signal, and he pranced away as if he had two loaves of bread tucked under his arms. Sally felt her body start to relax, just as she heard Michael toss over his shoulder, 'I guess we're not going for that drink any time soon?'

'Bastard,' Sally thought. Then she heard, 'I still miss my morning coffee, gorgeous.'

Mal's whole body turned to stone. Sally held his waist with both arms, staying him before he caused a scene. 'Who the hell was that dick?' Mal's eyes hadn't calmed any, nor did they stop throwing daggers at his opponent's back. 'Why the fuck did he have his hands on you? And what the fuck is he on about? Morning coffee? When did you have morning coffee with him, Sal?' He watched the intruder walk away and then turned to Sally; he looked down at her and saw the expression in her eyes. There was fright in them. Jaysus, he had made her frightened of him.

'Shit, sorry, babes, sorry.' He encircled her in his arms, holding her head tight against his chest. He was taking deep breaths, trying to calm himself down, and for a few moments, Sally stayed there knowing full well what they must look like to other customers passing. Closing her eyes, all she could see were Mal's nearly black beautiful eyes, but this time there was evil and hatred in them; she'd never seen it in him before and most certainly did not want to see it again. Michael was in the wrong, not her; she had done nothing to deserve that haunting look, and at that thought, she broke free from his arms and stormed off out the door of the shop. Her legs didn't move quick enough compared with the long stretch of his; he caught her around the waist and stopped her from moving.

Very quietly and calmly, she mouthed the words, 'Let me go.'

'Never!' he said back just as calmly. 'I am sorry, Sal. I just saw red when I saw that prick with his dick pressed against you.' Mal's jaw started to tick again, and Sally heard the grind of his teeth when he said the last four words.

'The way you looked at me was murderous, Mal. Me.' She pointed all ten fingers at her chest, tapping slightly. 'Why look at me like that? I did nothing wrong. I thought he was you, for God's sake.' Sally had tears in her eyes threatening to spill over by now and realised they were still in the middle of a shopping centre with people watching. Then a group of young fellas passed, saying, 'Take her to your car, at least, man.'

Mortified, Sally said, 'Let's go.'

'Did you get a dress?' Mal asked.

'No, am not in the mood now for some reason,' she spat at him.

'Come on.' Mal took her hand and walked quickly towards the glass exit doors of Foyleside. She skipped to keep up with him, but then he made a quick left towards the toilets, opened the door of the disabled toilet, dragged her in, and bolted the door before she had a minute to object. He pinned her to the wall with his hands on both sides of her face, his fingers stretching into her hair at the nape of her neck, his eyes now full of love and little flecks of panic; he kissed her with everything he had. After looking at the love and panic in his eyes, she thawed and kissed him back. He stopped the kiss, resting his head on her forehead. 'I told you I am going to make mistakes, Sal, but there's no way I will let the mistakes I make come between us. Nothing will ever come between us, Sal, you hear me?' He had to make her see he was just angry at that asshole, not her. He couldn't stand the thought of him feeling the pleasure of having Sally's ass pressed against his groin. The thought alone made his blood boil again and bile rise in his throat.

'You scared me, Mal. I thought it was me you were angry at.'

'Did you promise him you would go for a drink with him?'

'No, he's just a customer. He gets a bit flirty now and again, but he does it with everyone. He's harmless, Mal.'

'What I just saw wasn't harmless, Sal. He had his whole body pressed against you, the fucker.'

Sally put both her hands to his face now. 'It's only ever been you, Mal.'

'But . . .' Mal started to throw his toys out of his alpha male, big black leather twenty-two-inch alloy wheeled pram again, but she stopped him with a kiss – a big, wet, messy, full-on 'take-me-here-or-take-me-to-bed-very-quickly' kiss. They didn't however get a choice; the door handle wiggled and wiggled again. They were forced to break the kiss. Giggling nervously, Sally straightened herself as Mal mumbled something about a cold shower in order to be able to walk to the car. He took her hand and unbolted the door to a very grumpy-looking lady in a wheelchair.

'Sorry,' they both sang, still giddy from their kiss. Walking past River Island again, Mal asked if she wanted to go back in and get an outfit, but Sally give him a lustful 'you got to be joking' look, and he smiled a 'cat that got the cream' smile and off they trotted to the car.

Later that evening, after making up *a lot* (all new underwear sets got thumbs up, but the Merry Widow was definitely his favourite) after their first real fight, they both sat with their laptops out. Sally sat on the cuddle chair and Mal on the sofa; he was catching up on emails and Sally was making a second attempt at outfit shopping. After two new outfits, a dress and new shoes, she was done; she decided to text Nicole to ask if she was up for roller boots up the quay.

Fancy a fun workout? Xxxx

Deffs xxxx

C u at sains car park at 7? Xxxx

U will xxxx

'Am going up the quay with Nicole, babes. We are going out on our roller boots. It's been a while since we were out on them.'

'Righto,' Mal called back.

Sally gathered her roller boots and safety pads, and off she went, parked at Sainsbury's, and went in for a bottle of water. Michael was walking towards her on his way out.

'Hey, gorgeous, when you coming back to work?'

Sally was baffled. Did nothing faze this man?

'Hey, Michael, soon,' she said dryly, and away he went on about his business. She just shook her head as she went on with her purchase, listening and smiling to herself at the two girls at the counter discussing whether or not it was total bliss to take your bra off at night when you got in from work. One girl said it was and that she did it as soon as she got in the door. The other said her boobs were too big; she needed the support. They scanned Sally's water bottle and took money from her, laughing; one of the girls asked her what she thought. Sally thought it was definitely total bliss . . .

The girls had the best of craic on the roller boots as usual, but when Sally started to tell Nicole about her first fight with Mal on the way back down the quay towards their cars, Nicole had them stopping and starting every two minutes to get a certain part of the story repeated.

'And you call me drama-rama?' she shrieked. 'He's very dominant, Sally, isn't he?' Nicole's eyes were like saucers, her chin dipped and her head shook slightly.

'Yeah.' Sally couldn't help the pride in her voice as she said it. 'I kinda like it,' she giggled.

'You trollop, Sally May Mc Quire,' a stunned Nicole answered, earning herself a fun slap on the bum from Sally.

'Hey, so I got some new outfits for our break away. I just hope they come on time now.' Sally changed the subject.

'Am so looking forward to it, but it was a nightmare getting cover at the salon,' Nicole said.

Friday and Saturday being Nicole's busiest, Sally knew just how hard it would have been at short notice.

'Jeez, sure I am back at work on Monday, and I have to ask for a half day on Friday. The high and mighty Victoria isn't going to like that.'

Nicole snorted, adding, 'The bitch will be grand. I bet if you ask for a pay raise at the same time, she will give it to you after being without you for so long.'

Sally laughed, but she did hear that while she was off nursing Mal the café was opening late and closing early and that most days there wasn't even a full menu on. Victoria couldn't run a raffle, Sally knew that much.

'Anyway, Mal's rolling in the green stuff. You could afford to tell her to shove her job up her oversized nostrils.' Nicole flicked her own nose as she said it, but Sally was horrified.

'No way, Nicole, I could never live off a man.'

'I know, I know, keep your hair on. Speaking of hair, roots? Monday evening?'

Chapter 20

After a crazy few days shopping online for bits and bobs for the new house, Sally was glad for a little normality on Sunday evening. She was ironing her work uniform for Monday morning with a mixture of feelings. Spending mostly every hour with Mal the last two and a half months was amazing, and she could get used to it, but reality had to kick in at some stage. A seven o'clock start meant she was having an early night, so she bathed, de-fuzzed, body-buttered, and washed and blow-dried her hair. She went to cuddle on the cuddle chair for a little while. Mal was listening to John Legend on his iPhone.

'You smell fecking amazing, Sal.' Sally's Raspberry Body Butter was fast becoming Mal's favourite. Sally wiggled and giggled as he nipped and nibbled at her neck, then he pinned her under his body in one swift movement. Kissing was their second favourite thing in the world. 'Early night, you say?' Mal huffed out as he lifted them both off the chair and threw Sally over his shoulder effortlessly, swatting her bum as he strolled to the bedroom, kicking the door shut with his foot.

Six fifteen in the morning came early; the alarm went off, and Sally had to drag her ass out of bed and leave Mal all snuggled up and as warm as toast. This was going to be the longest time they would spend apart since reuniting (not counting Mal's injury time). She pouted, looking at him lying in bed; his tanned, toned, beautiful bared chest was an invitation, and his thick eyelashes fanned his cheeks, hair all messy and overlong, which made her think he hadn't had a hair cut since he came back other than the part the doctors cut to work at his head but even that was catching up with the rest now, she liked the length; she liked everything about him. She had to snap herself out of her lustful state and kick her own ass to the bathroom to ready herself for her day ahead. A quick shower, teeth brushed, and hair and make-up done and she was out the door at six fifty. 'Not bad going,' she thought to herself. Just as well it only took her between seven and nine minutes to get to work and park her car.

The café was a familiar sight and smell, and she fell back into her routine quickly. Her work colleague, Shelly, was opening up as she arrived. 'Hey, there, honi.' Shelly flung her arms around Sally and swayed her from side to side, her big boobs making Sally slightly uncomfortable as she was squashed into them, but it made Sally laugh too, and she realised how much she missed her work friends. Lisa came in at eight, hugged her, and welcomed her back too. They chatted away the most of the morning, Lisa filling her in on Victoria's absence and mess-ups of the rota. Shelly popped her head out through the service hole from the kitchen to the front counter, waving a vegetable knife and calling, 'I wouldn't get tired of slapping Vic's face with a big wet out-of-date trout.'

Sally and Lisa roared laughing; even the customers sitting, reading the morning papers, were looking at them and laughing at them laughing.

The phone rang at ten forty and it was Victoria checking if Sally had made it back in to work.

'Jeez, she took her time in checking, didn't she? All the bloody same, if you didn't make it in, we would have been short-staffed again. Like she even cares,' complained Lisa, wiping down a free table with a little more aggression than she normally had when talking about Victoria.

Tom the quiet, older gentleman came in and had a beaming smile on his face when he saw Sally. 'Welcome back, my dear,' he said in his well-mannered and well-spoken voice.

'Thank you, Tom,' she replied, setting up his tea, bread, and butter for one. 'It's nice to be missed.' Sally smiled at the old man, helping him load his tray and fill a milk jug.

'That you were, my dear. That you were.'

The rest of the day passed with 'welcome backs' and 'where the hell have you beens?' It flew in. Finishing time was four o'clock, and at ten to four, Mal breezed through the door, filling every inch of it. Sally noticed Lisa's eyes near popped out of her head before she noticed who she was looking at. Laughing out loud, she said, 'Put your tongue back in your mouth, girl. He's taken.' Then she approached him with her head tilted, ready for a kiss; she had been starved of him all day and wasn't at all shameful of the fact she was kissing him a little longer than she expected to.

Her day was hectic, but she had never stopped thinking about him for a minute. Lisa did not take Sally's advice; her tongue was still hanging out by the time the loved-up pair stopped acting like love-struck teenagers kissing. Sally burst out laughing at the sight of her and said, 'Lisa, this is Mal. Mal, Lisa.' Mal walked the distance to shake her hand, and Lisa reddened when she realised she had been gawking at him. 'I'm off, Lisa, see you tomorrow,' Sally called, still laughing at Lisa's reaction. When they were safely outside the front door of the café, she teased Mal, saying, 'You have an admirer, babe.'

'I only have eyes for you, babes.' He lifted her up to his mouth, and she threw her arms around his neck and snogged her man.

'I missed you like hell today, Sal.'

'I missed you too.'

'You're not going back. Am handcuffing you to the bed.' Mal's face was serious and his voice huffy. Sally, not sure if he was joking or not, she threw her head back, laughing but thinking she didn't even care if he wasn't joking.

'What you get up to today then?' Sally asked, waiting to hear all about Mal's first day without her. Mal stopped in the middle of the busy street, pulled his white long-sleeved top up past his chest, and revealed a tattoo. She gaped in surprise as she read the words permanently scrolled across his chest and over his heart.

Sal, you will
Forever
Be my
Always

'Oh, Mal.' She touched the writing on the word 'forever' that lay right on his heart. Mal winced, and she pulled her hand back swiftly, apologising. The next she heard was his husky laugh as he dropped his T-shirt over his taut tummy and lifted her again.

'You like it?'

'It's amazing, Mal. It's so . . . it's a . . . Jesus, you're not half wise, man.' She laughed, throwing her head forward into the crook of his neck and nipping him lightly in between her licks.

He told her to leave her car. It was a lovely day, and he wanted to walk the quay, so hand in hand they did just that. They chatted as they walked, hands swinging in between them. When they got to the Peace Bridge, Mal announced he had never been on the new bridge, so they walked that too, over to Ebrington.

Ebrington used to be an army parade ground back in the day, but was now dedicated to the arts; there was almost always some event held there now and even concerts. MTV even held their One Big Weekend there. At Christmas time, it was turned into a winter wonderland; at Halloween, it was a spooky horror town; and at Easter, an Easter egg hunt took place, but on an ordinary day, the space was a wonderland on its own, just lovely to walk around or just sit and people-watch.

They sat on a bench, and Mal got Sally a coffee at the pop-up vendor. Mal was well impressed.

'The city has come a long way from the dragon's teeth we used to sit on, sharing our lunch.' Mal kissed Sally's forehead as he sat beside her on the bench, handing over her coffee.

'It sure has. It's beautiful. I love Derry. We should walk the Walls sometime. I haven't done that in years. Dad used to walk Mum and me around them, telling us of their history. I didn't listen half as much as I wish I had now. We could do the Martin McCrossan city tour. It would be great listening to all their knowledge and stories of the siege and that.'

'Aye, that sounds like a plan, but only if we can do fake American accidents when we are asking questions.'

'You're a dork.' She swatted him on the shoulder, thanking the tattoo gods that it was the other side and not his inked side. She stood to make their way back, only to be swatted back on the bum.

'Will you quit with the bum?'

'Never.' *kiss*

'Ever.' *kiss*

Chapter 21

That evening Sally and Mal went to Nicole and Johnny's house. The boys had a few beers and watched four episodes of *Husbands of Hollywood* back to back; the girls had a few glasses of wine while Nicole took care of Sally's highlights. Mal was proud as punch to show off his new ink. Nicole called him an impulsive freak and warned Johnny to get his business up and running soon or he would be covered in the bloody things, she scolded. Johnny just laughed and took a closer look.

'Don't even think about it, Jonathan Cain White,' Nicole warned.

'Don't worry, honi. I'm a coward. I hate needles.'

Nicole touched Johnny's face. 'Aww, you're not a coward, baby. You're just sensible. Loads of *sensible* people don't like needles.' She kissed him on the nose.

'Kevin Hart is hilarious!' Mal was actually laughing and slapping his leg at the same time. Sally found herself laughing at Mal laughing. Johnny loved the series and had it recorded, but Mal hadn't heard of it, never mind seen it.

'I could watch this over and over again,' said Johnny.

'I love Robin Thicke in it,' Nicole said. 'His song about killing Kevin because he stole Paula is hilarious. Put that episode on, babes. Bet you, Robin has Paula's name inked on him too. He's just that crazy too.' Nicole laughed, looking at Mal and giving him a 'you know I love you really' look. Mal just laughed back at her and hugged Sally even tighter. The four of them got on so well, and Mal took a moment to appreciate his friends and most of all his life with Sally by his side, not a hair's breadth between them, physically or emotionally. As he gave a contented sigh, he heard Johnny announce he had found the right one, and the four of them laughed till they cried and then watched it over again.

Tuesday and Wednesday passed quickly; work was hectic and lots of customers welcomed her back and asked of her well-being.

Thursday morning, Victoria and two of her stuck-up friends came in for coffee – coffee with skimmed milk and scones with low-fat spread.

'Pain in the arses,' Sally mumbled as she turned her back on them to work the coffee machine.

Shelly popped her head through the service hole from the kitchen. In a low voice, she beckoned the girls close.

'If you two get Vic the tic back here, I could trap that hair of hers in the waste disposal for the craic. See how well she dances a desperate dance in those six-inch heels.'

'Oh my God, Shelly, you're soo bad,' laughed Lisa, shaking her head as she went back to preparing a fresh sandwich.

Sally snorted back her laughter, trying in vain to give Shelly a disapproving look.

Just before Victoria left, she called Sally into her office out back. The 'office', as she called it, had a cheap desk, cheap chair, phone, and a filing cabinet that Sally was pretty sure Victoria had no idea what was in there, never mind what to do with it all. '"A return to work" interview, Sally.' She nodded as if she knew what the hell she was doing.

'Ooo-K.' As Sally took a seat, she thought this was not what she had in mind. Victoria was full of shit, but she had no idea where this had come from.

'So you were sick?' she started.

Sally's brows pleated; she was shocked at this woman's pathetic behaviour and lack of respect for her. 'No, my boyfriend was in a bad accident, and I was off on compassionate leave.'

'Oh yes, yes, well, I can't pay you for someone else's sickness.'

'Ooo-K. Victoria, that's grand.'

Sally was beyond caring at this stage with Victoria's attitude towards her business and staff; it was a joke. 'Is that all?' Sally stood, now feeling impatient; if she didn't get out of there, she might do or say something that'd been coming a long time. Victoria stammered a little and stood herself.

'Yes, Sally, if that will be all, you can go.'

Sally's fury bubbled through her body and her head filled to boiling point. 'Bye.'

Sally lifted her coat and bag off the rack outside the office, took off her apron, and walked out the door. She decided to play Victoria at her own game, that game being 'who's a bigger bitch'.

'Where are you going?' Victoria called after her, panic in her annoying voice.

'Am sick!' she threw over her shoulder.

Chapter 22

*F*riday lunchtime, the four of them set off for Ballybofey, stopping for lunch at Doherty's café in Bridgend on the way. When they reached the hotel reception, a big red setter dog came wandering along the marble floor. He was old and seemed unfazed by them or anyone else passing. They could tell he was well used to people coming and going from the hotel, and it looked like he was part of the family, and it gave it a warm homey feeling. Then Sally noticed a sign saying: *Pet Friendly Hotel*; it all made sense. The dog settled itself at the foot of the hearth, where a big blazing open fire roared up the chimney.

They booked in, got their key cards from a very overly smiling receptionist, and made their way through the old original part of the hotel to the new building where their rooms were. The new building was a lot more extravagant with wide spacious corridors laid with a plush navy and gold carpet. It had contemporary art hanging on the walls and chaises lounges opposite them, as if they were to sit and admire. Large glass cases displaying lots of Irish designers' jewellery lined the corridors. Every piece was exclusive and quite affordable.

They left their bags in the rooms and arranged a time to be ready for dinner.

'First, you two are booked into the spa for "the works",' Johnny said with a gleam in his eyes, his hands holding up two fingers to make quotation marks. He knew the reaction he would get from Nicole, and she didn't disappoint.

'Yeah.' Nicole jumped into Johnny's arms with high-pitched octaves coming from her throat. Sally couldn't conceal her mirth either; she hugged her thoughtful man too, and they made their way down to the spa and leisure centre. Sally turned just before she exited their room and blew Mal a kiss.

The smell of chlorine faded as they entered the beauty suite and it was replaced with a mixed smell of vanilla, coconut, and lavender. They were handed chunky white bathrobes with the hotel logo, a stag, on the breast pocket, showed to the changing area, and were told to come through to the relaxation area when ready. This area had lounge chairs, magazines, daily papers, and a long fridge with bottled water and fruit with compliments. The girls went straight through for their massages. Two massage tables lay side by side. Tea lights in little glass holders were flicking everywhere on dark wood floating-shelves scattered around the top half of the walls; the soothing music that played softly set a relaxing tone. After full body massages, it was time for manicures and pedicures. They were handed flutes half filled with champagne, a strawberry on the side of the flute, and a bowl of freshly chopped exotic fruit salad each.

'Aww, this is the life.' Nicole clinked glasses with Sally.

'Cheers.' Sally clinked back.

'Here's to health and friendship.'

They clinked again and sipped their champagne and nibbled the strawberries on the side of the glasses. After their nails were buffed and polished to within an inch of their life, it was time for hair and make-up. Sally sat on the high director style chair for make-up and Nicole on the lower chair reserved for hair before swapping over in time for the other treatment. Nicole went for an up style with smoky enhanced eyes. Sally got a curly blow-dry and left her hair flowing down her back in soft waves just as she knew Mal liked it. She asked for her make-up to be done soft and natural. They looked stunning; just their outfits to slip into now and they were all set.

'I wonder what the boys got up to,' Sally said as they called the lift to the bottom floor to take them back to their waiting men.

'Umm, I hope they have not been propping up the bar all this time,' said Nicole as her eyebrow rose.

As they entered their rooms, the first thing they both noticed was that the boys had left a note for each of them. Nicole's read:

See you downstairs honi x

Sally's read:

Waiting downstairs babes xx

Sally got butterflies in her tummy. There was something romantic and exciting about the note and the thought of walking into the lobby and catching Mal's eyes scanning her body. 'It was like something out of a movie,' she thought on a giggle. She picked her dress with Mal in mind; she wanted to blow him away, and the little coral number with a very low-dipped back hopefully would do just that. When she checked herself in the full-length mirror, she was indeed impressed herself. It was so long since she had got dressed up and had full hair and make-up done. The colour of the dress went so well with her blonde curls falling around her shoulders and down her back; she wore silver strappy five-inch heels and silver jewellery and was ready to go. She gave herself a nod of approval and left to go get Nicole in the next room.

'Woot, woo,' said Nicole.

'Back at you,' said Sally.

Nicole wore a cream skater-style dress with gold heels and looked amazing. After telling each other how stunning they looked and having a wee excited girlie giggle to themselves, they made their way downstairs. Arriving at the reception area, they looked around a little but couldn't see the boys. Their notes were pretty vague. The hotel manager walked slowly towards them with a silver tray holding two glasses of champagne and two envelopes. He introduced himself as 'Amid' and handed the girls their bubbly and the mystery envelopes. The girls were confused slightly but minded their manners and thanked Amid as he walked away with a grin on his face. They both rested their flutes on the marble reception desk and opened the envelopes with as much haste as they could without ripping its contents. Both read the same in bold ink:

Follow the signs to the spa.

'Jeez, maybe they've seen us on CCTV and don't like our hair and make-up. Bet they want the girls to redo it all,' Nicole laughed. Then she added, 'Naw, of course, that's not it.' She said, flicking at her fringe slowly, 'Anyway Johnny wouldn't be that brave.'

Sally tended to agree with that but only silently. Heading towards the spa, they were still confused but really enjoying the excitement of the trail. They got to the staircase that would take them to the spa; they giggled and chatted, and by the time they reached the bottom stair, there stood Amid again with the same tray, holding two fresh champagne flutes and two more notes.

'What's going on, Amid?' Sally asked in a high pitched girlie voice. Amid just smiled, nodded, and walked off.

'Weirdo,' laughed Nicole, opening the new envelope. Both read the same in bold ink.

Meet you in the garden.

So off the girls went in search of the garden. When they spied a fire door with a laminated A4 sign saying 'GARDEN', they pushed the door out to the sound of the river Finn running along the garden of the hotel, and on the opposite side of the river was Drumboe Woods. Nicole was complaining about the grass being soft and that their heels would sink, but they followed a pathway through the garden. Cherry blossom trees lined the middle of a long but narrow garden, and at the end of it stood a huge white wooden gazebo with snowdrops and ivy crawling its way around the beautiful creation; little lantern lights looped around the roof of the gazebo, giving it a magical fairy-tale glow. It was stunning, but no sign of Mal or Johnny or Amid for that matter.

'What do we do now?' asked Nicole.

'Let's walk to the gazebo.'

Sally felt like she was being drawn to it; it was just too beautiful to deprive her eyes. She was so excited she could feel her whole body breaking out into goosebumps; she could feel her eyes dance in her head with anticipation. As they walked towards it, they could see candles flickering. They could hear music in the distance. They climbed the three wooden steps and stood in the middle, taking everything in; it was the most stunning sight, but even more stunning were Mal and Johnny appearing from both sides, both in three-piece suits. Johnny's suit was navy with a pale pink shirt and matching tie. Mal's was mid-grey with a crisp white shirt, the first two buttons undone; they stepped out of the shadows on each side, two huge big grins on their faces, and together they dropped to their knees and opened two small ring boxes.

'Marry me,' they both said in unison.

Nicole's squeal scared the birds out of the trees; she threw herself at Johnny, squealing. '*Yes*, oh my God, *yes*.' Johnny caught her in his arms and kissed her like his life depended on it. Sally was a little quieter but squealed nonetheless.

'Mal, I . . . I . . . can't believe you did all this.'

Mal nodded to the ring. 'Jeez, Sal, put me out of my misery here, babes.'

'Oh, oh, of course, I will, *yes*,' she squealed.

He slipped the platinum princess cut ring on her finger with ease and stood; snaking his arms around her waist, he lifted her up to his mouth.

'Baby, am gonna love you forever.' *kiss*

'And ever.' *kiss*

She finished his sentence with him, saying, 'And ever.' *kiss*

She kissed him with every emotion in her body . . . And there were *lot*s.

After snogging the life out of their romantic fiancés, Nicole and Sally hugged too and checked out each other's diamonds; Nicole's was a diamond teardrop, unusual and very pretty. Both girls were in a state of shock but buzzing with excitement.

From behind her, Mal wrapped Sally in his arms, saying, 'You look amazing, Sal. I can't believe how lucky I am.'

'Oh, Mal, I am soo lucky to have you. I love you *soooooo* much. Thank you for all of this.' She gestured around the garden and gazebo. 'It's amazing. I could never have dreamt of a better setting. It's like . . . like a fairy tale.' *kiss*

Nicole and Johnny were whispering their own sweet nothings to each other.

'It's not over yet, ladies,' Johnny said.

'There's more?' Nicole was clapping her hands like a two-year-old.

Mal raised his arm and called out, 'Amid!' The next thing they saw was a team of ten men and women carrying a table and four chairs, two ice bucket stands with champagne, cutlery, napkins, candles, and floral centrepieces. Then they were seated with their two men standing behind their chairs before they sat themselves and the music was now playing so they could hear it but just in the background. John Legend sang about being my end and my beginning; Sally's head was spinning with excitement, but she couldn't help tune into the words of the song, 'I am on your magical mystery ride'. 'That I definitely am,' Sally thought.

Nicole and Sally looked across the table at each other. Both pulled their shoulders up tightly and did an 'I can't contain my excitement' look and giggled.

The first course of cream of vegetable soup arrived, followed by bruschetta et cetera. Champagne was topped up, and they laughed and chatted amongst themselves. The main course was fillet of beef with garden salad and baby potatoes; sides of mash and tobacco onions were also produced. It was a feast, and four more could have joined them easily. The hotel staff were very polite and very attentive. Amid stopped by them after the main meal was devoured, asking if he could do anything for them. The night was perfect and the sun starting to set behind the trees of Drumboe Woods, and a chill had crept into the air. 'Your desserts will be served in your rooms,' Amid said proudly, and off he went.

Mal kissed Sally's hand and stood, whispering in her ear as he did, 'Alone time, baby.'

As they walked towards the lifts to make their way to their rooms, Johnny made the wrong choice of floors, and Sally corrected him only to be told by him that they had moved rooms.

'Why? The room we had was beautiful.'

Mal gave her a megawatt smile. 'Wait till you see this room.' *kiss*

Their new rooms were on opposite sides of the corridor on the same floor; the girls hugged and giggled some more and the men shook hands, but then thought better of it and man-hugged.

'All went to plan, thank God,' said Johnny, puffing out a long breath.

'Aye, thank God is right,' Mal laughed. 'Enjoy the rest of your night, you two.'

'Same to you both,' Johnny said, patting Mal on the back.

Sally's mouth fell open as she was led into the room; she was rendered speechless once again at the decor. One wall had a sheet of fairy lights covering the entire space. Floral arrangements dressed two mirrored console tables and the dining table which also had a pink tablecloth. A huge candelabra hung low from the ceiling over the middle of the table, with five pink church candles that flickered and danced in the reflection of the silver cutlery and mirrored furniture. It was all so romantic. The smell in the air was a mix of flowers and sweet scents. The cause of this was the huge chocolate fountain displayed between the two mirrored console tables. A selection of fruit, marshmallows, and fudge tempted Sally towards it; her mouth was watering at the sight and the smell. Mal took a stick, pierced a strawberry with it, dipped it into flowing chocolate, and fed it to her, then kissed and licked the chocolate from her lips. She returned the favour, wishing they were already in their bedroom. There was no bed to be seen, just the most amazing and romantic dessert room she could ever imagine. As if he had read her thoughts, Mal gave a crafty smile and pulled back a fan-like room-dividing door to reveal a beautiful white four-poster bed with pale pink dressing; pale pink posies sat on mirrored end tables with mini crystal chandeliers hanging over them, making the tables sparkle under the light.

'My heart can't take much more.' Sally shook her head in disbelief as she walked around the room in awe. 'When did you move all our things down here?' she asked, just noticing her overnight bag in the corner.

'Amid did it for us.' Mal stood in front of Sally and dipped for a kiss. 'Like some more dessert, baby?'

Sally snapped into dessert-room mode and looked up at Mal through her eyelashes.

'Yes, babes, and I hope *you* are in the mood for *a lot* more dessert.' *kiss*

'I have a very sweet tooth, Sal.' *kiss*

'Good.' *kiss*

'You?' *kiss*

'Yes. Very.' *kiss*

Unzipping her dress from the back and stepping out of it, she strutted towards the chocolate fountain again in just her lace panties and heels. She turned to face him; he was watching her every move, anticipation in his eyes for what was coming next. She ran her finger under the flowing chocolate and traced a very appetising line between her breasts, ending at her belly button, not taking her eyes off him the whole time.

'Oh, baby, you have no idea just how much more I want,' he said. In two swift strides, he was next to her, dipping his head to lick the line of chocolate between her breasts, starting at her belly button and making his way up and up slowly to her collarbone. He looked up at her with a cheeky grin and scooped her into his arms. As he turned towards the bed, he purposely dipped her toes into the chocolate. Sally let out a little yelp, and her head fell back laughing as her arms tightened around Mal's neck.

'I will start licking right there', he nodded to her toes, 'and I won't stop until I taste every inch of your body, baby.' Mal kept his promise and proved to have a *very* sweet tooth . . .

Chapter 23

Next morning, Sally woke up lying next to her fiancé, her legs curled around his. A smile spread across her face at the thought of the night before; she remembered everything in detail, and she looked to her left hand, checking out her rock – one solid square diamond with lots of small diamonds standing guard all the way around it. She couldn't have picked better herself. Mal woke, stretching out his long legs and pulling her close to him.

'Morning, beautiful.'

'Morning yourself, sexy,' she replied, kissing his chest and up to his neck.

'My girl wants more chocolate for breakie, eh?' Mal pinned Sally under him, taking over the kiss.

'I think my teeth may rot if I eat any more.' Sally giggled and wiggled as he nipped and nibbled her neck.

'Shall we speak with Amid today about booking this hotel for our wedding? He was great and couldn't do enough for Johnny and me when we were organising all this.'

Sally thought for a moment. 'I should ring Mum and Dad first before we go booking hotels, but yeah, this hotel is perfect, and it would be a shame to go anywhere else now after what happened here last night.' Sally couldn't help the wide smile on her face and taking a quick look at her ring.

'I asked them both weeks ago,' Mal spoke casually, 'your parents, I mean, way before the accident. I knew what I wanted, Sal, even before I got back, so there was no point waiting about.'

'No, you certainly don't wait about, babes. What would you have done if I had been with someone?' she laughed.

'Don't joke about that, baby. That was my worst fear.' His eyebrows were knotted as if in pain at the very thought. 'But I would have crushed the poor bastard. Am addicted to you, Sal. I need you to live. Am living now, but I wasn't before. I was just existing. It's like the last ten years were meant to be, just so we could have this, here now.' *kiss* 'I adore you,' he continued. 'I promise to worship you until I take my last breath, Sal. I want to be your everything, the centre of your whole world.'

'Mal,' she breathed, her whole body feeling like chocolate melting into his hot, muscular body. Her heart beating fast in her ears and her breath catching, she answered, full of love and emotion, 'You, my babe, already have that ticked.' *kiss*

When Sally recovered from Mal's words and *kiss*es, she got up to make the call to her parents. It was only then she noticed the bedcovers. It had chocolate and strawberry juice stains all over them.

'Oh, Mal.' She was horrified. 'How we will explain these stains? This is sooo embarrassing.'

'Sal, I think they might be expecting something like this. I did propose to you last night, and given what the room was reserved for.' He shrugged. 'Dessert.'

He grabbed her wrist and yanked her back to bed. She was giggling and wiggling again, as he rolled to put her under his chest.

'I think I requested handcuffs to be left in here. Wait till I look.'

Sally's eyes nearly popped out of her head until Mal laughed his head near off at her expression. She slapped him on the shoulder and got up to ring her mum and dad, receiving a slap on the ass for good measure. Elizabeth's squeal was deafening. Mal heard it from the bed when Sally had to hold the phone away from her ear.

'Oh, darling, we are delighted for you both and, of course, Nicole and Johnny.'

Sally came and sat on the bed beside Mal, and he took her left hand and pulled it to his lips; once again Sally's heart skipped a beat. John's was the next voice Mal heard chat to Sally.

'Congratulations, pet. I know you will both be very happy.'

'Thanks, Daddy.' Sally's eyes filled up at her dad's words for some unknown reason. 'Sorry, I guess am just overwhelmed. I can't wait to show you and mum my ring.'

'Love you, pet. Here's your mum again.' Sally chatted to her mum, filling her in on the details of the hotel trail and the beautiful gazebo, leaving out the dessert room for obvious reasons. She promised to call at her mum's as soon as they got back on Sunday to show off her diamond.

Breakfast came to their room at ten fifteen. Sally was in the shower and came out to another feast on the dining table. Mal had a fry-up and tea, but Sally opted for fruit, croissants, and a coffee. Then back to bed it was after a quick call to Nicole and Johnny's room while Mal took his shower. Nicole was as expected, still on a high.

'I had to try really hard to talk my mum and dad out of driving down here to see us,' Nicole told Sally. 'Mum was so excited and wanted to give me a big hug and be the first to see the ring.'

Sally laughed, saying, 'That's soo Anna.'

While Elizabeth was just as excited for Sally and Mal, she wouldn't want to land herself in the middle of their time together on this special weekend, but Anna was the opposite; she just loved to be in the middle of the drama (Nicole didn't get it off the back of a bus).'

She is ringing Elizabeth now to sort out arrangements for dinner or something tomorrow when we get back.'

'Great, but they better not expect us too early,' Sally warned, knowing full well Anna will be dishing out orders for times and places and she did not want to be on a schedule this weekend above all.

At twelve o'clock, Nicole rang their room, wanting to know if they fancied a swim. They all decided a swim and sauna would be great. The pool was packed with kids and their parents, so they decided on the Jacuzzi first. They sat relaxing in the bubbles with only Nicole's voice to be heard, trying to make up her mind as to whether she should go away to get married or do it at home.

'Want to go for a steam, Sal?'

They left Johnny listening to Nicole's drama on his own. Sally sat on Mal's lap in the steam room, their bodies slippery against each other.

'I would never tell or ask you to do anything you didn't want, Sal, but please, please tell me you don't want to make it a double wedding.'

'I hadn't even considered it. I think it should be our day, babes. I mean the proposal was amazing, and it was great we could share it with Nicole and Johnny, bu—'

Taking her mouth in relief, he kissed her hard and long, breaking the kiss to say, 'I love Nic, but jeez, there's only so much a man can take. I don't know how Johnny does it.' He laughed.

'Aww, she's a doll. She just loves the drama, that's all.'

She moved with a quick slip of her legs and straddled him, kissing him some more.

'Jeez, Sal, not that I am complaining or anything, but if someone comes in here I won't be able to hide my excitement, babes.' He nodded downwards.

Laughing, she gave him one last wee teasing roll of her hips and got off his lap and, of course, got a slap on the ass as she did. When the pool got quieter, they went for a quick swim before heading back up to their rooms to get ready for their last evening at Jackson's.

'Dinner and dessert at the table?' pouted Sally. 'Tut-tut,' she said, leaning into Mal when the dessert menu was handed to her.

It took Mal a minute to realise what she was pouting about, and then he laughed and raised an eyebrow at her, saying, 'don't tempt me, baby.'

Knowing full well Mal wouldn't think twice about lifting her from the table, throwing her over his shoulder, and ordering dessert in their room on the way out of the restaurant, she smiled into her menu and kept quiet.

Conversation flowed as did the wine and beer for the boys; their laughter filled the restaurant, although they tried their best to be as respectful as they could to the other diners. An older couple in their seventies passed their table on their way out of the dining room. Sally had noticed them looking at them every now and then throughout dinner but with a smile on their faces. The man stopped at their table and leant in slightly, saying, 'Enjoy your youth, my friends. You know, you four remind my good wife and myself of many moons ago. We had two good friends too and dined and holidayed together and laughed just like you four are tonight.'

'Aww,' the two girls sang in unison.

'I bid you four good night and much laughter together.' The man's hand was waving in the air and his wife was smiling a wide, full toothy smile but was quite shy.

'Good night' was all she spoke and off they went. Mal, Johnny, Nicole, and Sally called good night after them.

'It's hard to think of us at that age,' said Johnny, lifting his pint glass. 'To growing old together.' He raised his glass in a toast.

'To growing old together.' They all toasted.

'I am going to make a promise right now.' Nicole was tapping her finger on the table. 'If I ever see anyone worthy of those same words that man has just said to us, I will approach them when am old and grey, maybe not grey, and say the very same words, but only if they are worthy now.' Nicole was wagging her finger and starting to slur a bit.

'Do you want me to write the words down for you, babes, so you can keep them safe for the worthy recipients?'

'Aww, tanks, babes, would ye?' Nicole said gratefully, looking at Johnny, all starry-eyed.

Mal and Sally both nearly wet themselves laughing at Nicole and Johnny, their cuteness, and how well they worked together.

'You two are made for each other,' Mal said, as Sally mumbled through her laughing, 'My jaws are too sore laughing. Will you two stop?'

They went dancing after dinner. They were already feeling the buzz of the alcohol, so the girls went straight to the dance floor for a bop. The boys went to the bar and then scanned the room for a seat. Two girls sat beside them so quickly Mal thought they had been going for the same seats and just arrived at the same time.

'Hey,' one of the girls slurred, breathing her boozy fumes up into Mal's face. The other was dancing between Johnny's legs, like she was a stripper earning her night's wage. Johnny's mouth fell open for a second or two before he pulled his legs up and did a quick side jump over the back of the couch. Mal howled, laughing at Johnny's reaction and the girl's face. One minute she was pulling her sexiest moves on a fella she had pinned to the seat with her curves and the next he was gone. It took the harlot a few seconds to work out where he had got to, which just made Mal laugh even more.

'Run along now girls,' Mal shooed them away, laughing, but with the least bit of tolerance for the duo. Johnny blew out a breath as he sat back down, shaking his head at his close encounter with the nearest thing to a stripper he had ever got to. The music was loud, and Mal couldn't stop laughing long enough to make sense while he relayed the story to the girls on their return. But when he finally got it out, Sally laughed as much as he did, but Nicole was horrified. She patted Johnny's face with the back of her hand, asking if he was OK. She was deadly serious. The thought of her poor Johnny being attacked by that hussy made her glue herself to his side for the rest of the night. Poor Johnny was still in shock, and the next round was Double Jacks and Coke for the boys. Anything to try and bring Johnny round . . . The rest of the evening buzzed into a blur . . .

'Hangover, baby?' Mal stood over her as fresh as a daisy, showered, shaved, and smelling divine.

'Wee bit.' Sally's throat was dry and her voice croaky; her eyes were squinting to adapt to the light.

'We have to check out in an hour and breakfast has just arrived.' *kiss*

Mal placed sparkling water and two headache tablets on the mirrored end table beside her. Elbowing her way up the bed, she said, 'Great, I will never come round in time.' When her head reached an upright position, she felt the full impact.

'Oh my God!' she complained and flopped back down on the pillow and pulled the blankets up around her head.

Mal pulled the blankets from her, lifted her in his arms, her head resting on his shoulder, and walked to the bathroom. He placed her on the marble counter around the sink and ran cold water on a facecloth, then held it to her face, softly wiping her brow, then her cheeks.

'Better?'

She nodded, and he handed her, her toothbrush with paste on it and left her to it.

After breakfast and a bucket load of coffee, she came round, and when they met Nicole and Johnny in the corridor outside their rooms, Nicole looked like Sally felt.

'Oh dear, living light, I think I drank my body weight in wine last night,' Nicole complained, putting on her sunglasses.

'Amid was on the phone this morning, Nic. He wants payment for the marks your high-heel things left on the bar last night,' Mal teased Nicole.

Her mouth fell open, but she was speechless; then she turned to Johnny as if it was his fault.

'Johnny!'

'He's taking the piss, honi.'

Mal walked away, laughing, and Nicole slapped him, saying, 'I think I just threw up in my mouth, Malacey Quinn.'

'When will you learn, baby?' Johnny laughed but rubbed Nicole's back in a caring, loving gesture.

The girls ordered sparkling water in the hotel lobby as the boys checked out and chatted to Amid.

Sally watched Johnny shake Amid's hand and then Mal did the same; she saw a bank note or three slip into Amid's hand and an even bigger smile grow on his face. When they finished their drinks, they set off for home.

Chapter 24

Elizabeth was standing at the front window, waiting. When they pulled up, she darted out the front door and scooped Sally in her arms, actually lifting her a little off the ground.

'Oh, darling, I am so delighted for you both. Let me see, let me see.' She was groping for Sally's left hand. 'Oh, it's beautiful, darling. Come in, come in.'

'They can't get in past you, Elizabeth,' laughed John, coming to the door to greet them. Elizabeth was still holding Sally, so John extended his hand to Mal and pulled him in for a slightly awkward hug. 'Congratulations, Mal, take care of my baby girl now.' John slapped him on the back.

Mal made his way for a hug from Elizabeth, and Sally got a grizzly bear hug from her dad. Inside, Elizabeth informed them of Anna's plans for dinner to celebrate the engagements. All eight of them and both dads took the next day off work so they could relax and enjoy the night without worrying about getting up in the morning. Anna had phoned Johnny's parents, but they declined the offer of dinner, saying it was too long a drive at night. Elizabeth spoke of all the plans as she opened a bottle of champagne and poured four glasses. Sally took two or three sips from hers for a toast and then left it.

'Am going to save myself for tonight, I think.'

'I am so excited for you both. Have you thought of what kind of wedding you would like, Sally?' Elizabeth asked. Sally and Elizabeth chatted about Jackson's Hotel and how great the staff had been over the weekend. The men sat chatting about the latest up-and-coming boxer and when his next fight was.

Da Vinci's Restaurant was quite busy, but their table was reserved on a little stage-like area. It had two huge free-standing candelabra with at least fifteen candles in each on both sides of the table and a very impressive floral arrangement; it looked beautiful and very romantic. The champagne was chilling in two ice buckets, and the waiters were standing at the ready to seat them. They definitely pulled out all stops for them. Dinner was just as impressive, and the company was perfect too. Sally and Nicole had not talked about the elephant in the room, being the fact that they were going their separate ways for their weddings, but it became obvious as Nicole was already talking about going to Greece and marrying on a beach and how Johnny was going to wear white and they both would be barefoot on the sand and how romantic it was going to be. Of course, Johnny just buzzed off Nicole's excitement.

Mal was never as glad to hear Nic say 'my wedding' as in her and Johnny instead of 'our wedding' as in the four of them. The evening was going great. Mal went to use the gents, and when he returned, he looked flushed. Sally put her hand on his knee and asked if he was feeling OK, but he dismissed her concerns. As the night went on, Mal got more closed off from their company. Sally put it down to him being tired and not fully back to himself after the accident.

They declined the offer to go back to Anna and Jim's house for drinks. They kissed, hugged, thanked everyone, and got a taxi home together.

'You OK, Mal? You look like you've seen a ghost,' Sally asked him when they got into bed that night.

'I'm just tired, babes.'

Victoria called Sally on the Monday morning.

'Are you feeling better, Sally?' Her fake sweet voice came over the phone.

'I am feeling a bit better, Victoria. I will be back at work on Thursday.'

'Thursday?' she shrieked.

'Yes, Thursday.' And Sally hung up.

They were getting the keys to their house the next day, so she wanted a few days off for that. Victoria was the last person she wanted to talk to or see for that matter, so she turned her phone off once she hung up on her. She would deal with her on Thursday. Mal was out and about, she wasn't sure what he was doing but assumed it was business, but Sally took the time to box up some things and sort through her wardrobes. The whole day went by her, but she got through a lot of sorting and boxing. When she noticed the time and realised her phone was switched off, she panicked a bit because Mal hadn't been in touch or been home all day. She switched on the phone, and a text beeped through.

Got meetings all day babes c u tonite x

She relaxed instantly, sending him a text right back.

Miss u xx

Mal brought dinner home with him, and they sat on the sofa watching reruns of *Friends*. When Sally mentioned renting the apartment out to Betty Mc Carron's daughter, Chloe, Mal thought it was a great idea, so Sally texted Anna for her number, then rang Chloe. They arranged for her to call and see the apartment the next evening. Sally came off the phone smiling at the girl's excitement. Mal was so tired that night he fell asleep before Sally even got into bed after her bath, so she just cuddled up to him and planted light kisses on his chest.

Kisses were what she woke to the following morning.

'Morning, beautiful. Today's the day.' *kiss* 'We get our keys.' *kiss*

'Yeah!' said Sally, beaming before she had even opened her eyes. Mal stood to get dressed, and she bounced out of bed and into his arms, wrapping her legs around his waist and hugging him tight.

'Am sooo excited. The house is just beautiful, and I can't wait to make it our home.' *kiss*

Mal put her on her feet, slapped her ass, and said, 'Get dressed, beautiful. Let's go get those keys.'

The drive to the solicitor's office took them ten minutes. Sally chatted about their new furniture and which days each item would arrive, but Mal was distant and quiet. Sally put it down to him being worn out from all his meetings yesterday and made a mental note to chat to him about not doing too much. 'His brain is still recovering, and he needs to remember that,' she thought. They spent a half an hour in the solicitor's office signing their names and chatting; then they walked back to the car, Sally swinging the key chain around her ring finger as she walked. They drove straight to Sea Mist, texting her mum and dad on the way.

Got the keys. Yeah. Call round to c it xx

Sally got a text right back.

Yeah. Give us an hour xx

It was a late summer glorious day, and as they drove up the drive to their new home, the colours in the garden were glorious too. Sally's breath caught, and her heart was thumping with excitement. Mal put the key in the door and turned to Sal. 'Welcome home, baby.' *kiss*

'Am gonna make you soo happy, baby.' *kiss*

'Am gonna love you forever.' *kiss*

He opened the door to a hallway filled with flowers and balloons. There were at least twenty-four-foot tall vases, each filled with different flowers: lily of the valley (return of happiness), honeysuckle (devotion), fuchsias (humble love), daffodils (new beginnings), and red and orange roses (love and fascination); every vase was mixed with baby's breath (everlasting love).

'Nic helped with the flowers,' Mal admitted. 'Well, when I say helped, she more or less ordered me to buy these ones. Jeez, she takes it all so serious, doesn't she?' he laughed.

'Oh, they're beautiful.' She threw herself into his arms, bursting with happiness and planting kisses all over his face. 'Thank you, oh, thank you, babes.'

'And look.' Mal nodded to the kitchen window, the one above the sink, to their cactus plant taking pride of place already. 'Nicole insisted that it be the first thing to be moved in.' Mal rolled his eyes but laughed with Sally.

Laughter and love just filled the house, and Elizabeth and John could hear and feel it as they popped their heads around the door.

'This house is amazing, darling.' Elizabeth was in awe as she scanned the room, they were both well impressed. Sally was on cloud nine showing her mum and dad around; Mal just buzzed off her. The house echoed as they walked from room to room, and as they walked back towards the hallway, the smell of flowers was thick in the air. They ended the tour in the kitchen, and Mal produced champagne from the fridge and flutes from the cupboard. As instructed by Mal, the solicitor had left everything ready for them to toast their new home.

John held his flute in the air and toasted, 'To Sally and Mal and their new home and future together . . .'

Chapter 25

Over the next two weeks, the furniture arrived piece by piece, and the spare bed got set up in the spare room, and for now, that was where they would sleep until Mal got his business set up and made them a bed and furniture himself. Sally decided to stay off work and let Victoria stew. She ordered fresh rose petals and rose-scented candles and was to pick them up on Friday morning. Friday was to be their first night under their new roof, and it had to be just perfect. Mal was quite stressed out and distant since the celebratory dinner. When Sally asked him if he was OK, he would just brush her concern off, and when she asked about his meetings and buying days, he just dismissed the questions with 'Just a meeting, Sal.' Sally worried about his health, but she thought once they moved in, things would get better.

There were enough rose petals ordered to make a trail from the front door up the stairs into the bedroom, dress the bed, and then extra to sprinkle on top of the water in the huge free-standing bathtub if and when needed. New underwear was on order, and she was booked in for a spray tan and hair and make-up; she was all good to go. Mal was out and about all week, in and out of meetings and buying machinery for his business. She hardly saw him; she missed him, and he was always so tired when he got home. Worry was starting to take over the excitement, worry that he might be taking too much out of himself.

Everything was boxed up and ready to be put in the boot of their cars as she was leaving all her furniture in the apartment for Chloe. On Friday morning, she kissed Mal on her way out to prim and prime herself for the night to come. They arranged to meet at Sea Mist for dinner at six. Mal was taking care of dinner, and all Sally had to do was turn up all beautiful and hungry . . .

Sally dropped the key off with Chloe's mum, and off she went to spend the best part of the afternoon with Nicole at her salon.

'You look stunning, Sally.' Nicole was so proud of her and her staff for the makeover. Sally's hair was left glossy and falling in soft waves, her make-up seductive but classy, and her skin glowing with a healthy light tan. She felt great too. She left Nicole's salon on a high, her head filled with thoughts of rose petals, dinner, her stunning house, and a very perfect fiancé.

After picking up the rose petals and candles, she stopped and bought a bottle of Prosecco and a box of chocolates, thinking she would go back to the apartment and leave them there for Chloe as a 'welcome to your new home' gift. Hoping Mal still had his key for the apartment, she rang him, but his phone went straight to voicemail. She would just have to go back to Chloe's mum and ask for the key back for half an hour. That done, she set off to the apartment, parked up, and went to the boot of her car to grab a handful of petals to sprinkle around the chocolates and Prosecco. She turned to walk towards the apartment but got nowhere. Mal was standing just outside the double glass doors with his hand on the bottom of a girl's back, and he just dipped and kissed her on the cheek, a goodbye kiss. Sally's head spun full circle.

'A goodbye kiss,' she thought.

'Goodbye from my apartment?'

'Goodbye after what?'

Her legs moved before her brain, but they decided to carry her back to the door of her car, and she slid into the driver's seat and watched them chat some more, laugh, and look into each other's eyes. The girl was slim and tall, with dark brown bobbed hair, all shiny and soft, but she couldn't see her face, so she didn't know how old she was. But judging by the figure-hugging red dress she was wearing, she was about Sally's age, maybe younger. Maybe it was someone from Madrid, followed him back to Derry; she did look kinda Spanish from the back. Sally's blood started to boil after the shock subsided. She thumped and thumped the steering wheel.

'I knew this was all too good to be true. How could I be so stupid?' she was spitting out through her clenched teeth. She took her phone out and snapped three photos before it got too much and the tears started, as she watched the girl put her hand on his forearm and squeeze it a little and then laugh, throwing her head back, all flirty. Sally watched his lips say something like 'I will call you.' She was deflated. She could feel every bit of life slowly leave her body; she was frozen to the spot, numb and sad, a sad, pathetic excuse for a woman for falling all over again for Mal Quinn and all his bullshit sweet talk. She saw him disappear back upstairs to the apartment. She looked down, and the rose petals were mush in her lap. Her phone rang; it was *him,* but she couldn't talk to him. She couldn't think straight, so she just listened to it ring and then ring again, but on the third ring, she decided to answer and ask where he was.

'Hello.'

'Hello babes, what you at?'

The bastard sounded 'full of the joys of spring'.

'I just finished up in Nicole's salon. What you up to?'

'I just finished a meeting in town with a solicitor about the unit, going to sort dinner out now. Hope you're hungry.'

'Yes, am hungry.'

'You OK, babes?'

'Yes, it's a bad line. See you shortly.'

She hung up. Anger bubbled through her. She drove straight to a chemist and printed out all three photos. Then she drove to the new house, took the petals from the boot, lay them in a trail from the front door to the bottom of the stairs, then to the bedroom. She went back to the car for the candles, lay them on the plush cream and gold carpet of the bedroom floor, and took her wedged heel shoe to them, smashing them all and venting her anger at the same time, but for only a short time. She ripped up two of the photos just enough so he could still make them out and laid the third photo on the bed with a few rose petals scrunched into mush beside it.

'Fuck you,' she spat and turned on her heel and walked out the front door of her dream home and out of Mal's life. The last few weeks ran through her head – his distance, always being tired, and there she was worried about his health, while he was off banging his Spanish lover. The lying, cheating bastard! Tears stung her eyes now even more than ever, her entire body was vibrating with anger. She had nowhere to go. It would be much too hard to tell anyone what she'd seen and admit what a stupid lovesick gullible fool she had been. Her phone rang again and again. Both were Mal, but she couldn't face talking to him; the scene at the house would tell him all. She booked herself into a hotel and cried and cried and cried into her pillow.

Mal pulled up to the house, disappointed Sally wasn't there already, but he knew it was for the best because he wanted to dress the table and set everything out. His solicitor had put him in touch with a chef, and he was preparing a feast for them – oysters to start with and Mal's favourite, fillet of beef with all the trimmings; he was even supplying a chocolate fountain for afters. The chef was to prepare the fruit for dipping and all was being delivered in a half an hour. He had showered at the apartment and dressed in Sally's favourite, one of his many white shirts and jeans. All was going to plan; all he needed was his girl in his arms. He opened the door and spied the trail of rose petals; he smiled like the cat that got the cream. He followed them to the bedroom and nearly vomited.

First he thought something had happened to Sally when he saw the candles smashed to bits; then he saw the photos. His heart dropped to his stomach, and he turned and ran out of the house to the car, where he had left his phone. He rang Sally's number repeatedly, but no answer; then after the fourth ring, it was switched off. 'Shit. Shit. Shit.' He rang Nicole. 'You see Sally?'

'Hello to you too, Mal . . .'

'Nic.' His warning voice gave Nicole the shivers.

'What's wrong, Mal? She was here earlier, but I haven't seen her since.' He hung up. Elizabeth's phone rang off, so Mal decided she was with her. He drove like a bat out of hell until he got to Elizabeth's house, but there was no one there. With his phone up and down to his eardrum, frantically phoning between Elizabeth's number and Sally's, he was like a caged animal, pacing up and down Sally's parents' drive. No answer, so he rang John's phone.

'John, heard from Sally?'

John could tell Mal was stressed. 'No. What's going on, Mal?'

'She misunderstood a situation, John, and now I can't find her. Where the hell would she be? Do you know where Elizabeth is?'

'Elizabeth is right here with me. You better come here, Mal, and tell all so we can help find her.'

John wasn't asking; he was telling Mal. Mal could do with all the help he could get to find her, so he went to John's office.

Sally spent her night crying; she had ordered a bottle of wine to her room, finished it, and ordered another one, telling herself it was just to make sure she slept. She had left her phone in the car so she wouldn't be tempted to switch it on and listen to Mal's lies. Morning came with a bang on the head and her heart. Today she would have to deal with him. He had most likely rung everyone trying to find her and her mum and dad would be worried sick. She got up, showered and dressed, skipped breakfast, and checked out. She went to her car. Her hand was shaking; switching on the phone, there were twenty-six voicemails, and the texts just kept beeping in constantly. She listened to three voicemails from Mal.

'Sally, answer your phone please, babes, I need to explain.'

'Sally, will you please answer the bloody phone?'

'Sally! You are behaving like a spoilt teenager. Answer the fucking phone.'

She had heard enough. She switched the damn thing off again. She just sat there worrying about where she was going to live now, when she realised this was not her fault and this was his doing. She decided she was going home; he could fuck off to the B&B he came from before she took him home to her apartment, the apartment in which he entertained his Spanish slut. She drove with her nostrils flaring and her heart racing. His car wasn't to be seen, so she parked hers and went inside and straight upstairs. She fixed her hair and make-up, put on a red dress, then thought better of it, because 'Miss Spanish lover' had worn one. She changed into a green skater-style dress and nude wedges and went downstairs to wait for him to come back, and then she would throw him out again. It was then she noticed the kitchen table was upside down and the chairs lying all over the kitchen floor were in splinters. He must have taken the frustration of being caught out on the table and chairs; then she noticed fist prints on the doors leading to the kitchen and utility room. She started to feel uncomfortable, and the buzz in her ears blocked the noise of the front door opening and Mal flinging himself into the kitchen.

'Sal, thank God you came home.' He pounced on her, grabbing her to his chest, and for a few seconds, she froze.

'Get the hell off me.' She punched at his chest.

'Will you just listen to me, Sal?' He held on to her arms tight.

'What? Listen to your bullshit excuse for banging your Spanish slut in *my* apartment? I don't think so, Mal. Now get your hands off me.'

She was like a crazy woman bombarded with emotions of disgust and humiliation and deceit. Mal was in shock; he'd never seen Sally like this before.

'Sally, I have a surprise for you.'

'What? What? You deluded bastard, you think you can throw money at me and I will forgive you? Get out, *get* the *fuck* out.' Her tears were flowing fast now, and Mal wrapped his arms around her, pulling her into his hard chest as she fought him with every emotion and every bit of fight she had in her.

'You stupid woman,' he spat out and carried her kicking and screaming to the living room; he threw her on to the sofa and pinned her there by holding her arms tight against her legs with all his strength.

He knelt over her, looking down into her emerald eyes, saying, 'Do you really think I could do that to you, Sal?'

Sally screamed at the top of her voice, 'I saw you, Mal. I saw you with my own eyes, and I even have the photos to prove it. You lying, cheatin—'

'You saw what? Me talking to a girl, a girl who—'

She cut him off, trying to flip him from her. 'I don't want to know who the hell she is. Now get the hell off me.'

'Sally, please just listen to me, will you? I want to let you sit up, and I want us to talk like adults about this. Will you do that if I let you up?'

Breathing heavily, she agreed. Her mind was on overdrive, but most of all, painful stabbing daggers were swooping through the air and into her heart, lungs, and tummy. Her breathing was heavy, but it hurt. Her body on the outside was rigid, but inside it was like mush. Her eyes hurt just looking at his pained but stunning face; his brown eyes were so adorable she was starting to melt. Desperately, she fought for the fading resentment and put the mentally devastating image to the front of her mind. The minute he was off her, she ran. She ran upstairs and locked herself in the bathroom, suddenly not wanting to talk to him *or* fight with him; she just wanted to be alone, nurse her heart and cry again. Mal knocked at the door and nearly put the bloody thing through with his fists.

'Go away, please, Mal.' Her voice was small and weak now, and that just broke Mal's heart even more.

'Sal, did you not recognise the girl?'

Sally didn't answer; she just froze to the wall that she had slid down against, between the bathtub and the sink. 'Sal? It was Victoria. How did you not notice it was your boss?'

Sally's breath left her body, and she had to make herself breathe in again; she couldn't believe it. Victoria, her bitch self-righteous boss, was having an affair with *her* Mal. Then she realised the girl's hair was a short bob. Victoria's hair was waist-length. Her head was in a spin with lies and more lies.

'That wasn't Victoria, Mal,' she sniffed.

'Yes, it was, babes.'

'Don't you babes me. So if it is Victoria, are you telling me you're having an affair with her? How thoughtful of you to pick someone I already *fucking* hate.' Venom was slicing through her veins now; she was shocking herself with her vulgar language.

'Sal, open the door please.'

'No. Get lost.'

All of three seconds passed until the door was kicked in and Mal had Sally in his arms again, attempting to restrain her once more. She was lifted and pinned to the wall, this time by six feet four inches of muscle. With one hand, he held her face up to look at him.

'Look at me, Sal. Look at me, *damn you. I bought the fucking café for you*, you silly woman.'

A staring contest started until everything he had said sunk in; he still kept her pinned until he felt her body relax.

'You did what?' was all she could manage to whisper slowly.

'I-bought-the-café-for-you. I was going to give you the signed paperwork last night at dinner.' Sally's head pounded now with a new tension.

'Why the apartment? But she had long hair.' Sally couldn't get a proper sentence together.

'I don't know shit about the woman's hair, but I didn't have time to meet her at the solicitor's office at the time she suggested, so I texted her to come to the apartment when I knew you would be out for the day. I needed the signed paper to make moving-in night the best it could be or, at least, the best I thought it would be. This is all such a big fucking misunderstanding, Sal.'

He felt her body relax more as he slackened his hold on her, but he wasn't letting go completely.

'Why did you feel the need to kiss and touch her then?'

Mal screwed his face in disgust. 'She's a stuck-up cow, and I wanted something from her, her business *for you*. I was just keeping her sweet, Sal, charming her into signing the papers, that's all.'

'Mal, am . . . I . . . I don't know what to say.'

He put his hands on either side of her face, his long fingers stretching into her hair and holding her secure.

'Thank you. You could say thank you, babes.' *kiss*

'Am so sorry, Mal.' *kiss* 'Thank you so much.' *kiss*

Mal held her tight as she started to sob again, but at the realisation that she was wrong, not that he was a fake and a liar.

'I can't believe I put myself through all this and you were only doing something nice for me.'

'Put *yourself* through it? Jeez, Sal, I was going out of my mind. Your mum and dad are going nuts too with worry.'

He took his phone out of his pocket and sent John a text.

She's home. All's good.

'Mal, am so sorry. I ruined moving-in night. I am so sorry, babes, am so, so sorry.'

Mal pushed his fingers through his hair, stopping at the nape of his neck, his elbows pointing towards her face.

'I can't believe you would think that of me, Sal, that I would do that to you, and just two weeks after I proposed to you. I bought this house, the café. Everything is for *you*, Sal. If you're happy, am happy. Why can't you just trust me? What else do I have to do for you, Sal?'

In one swift movement, he ripped his shirt open, buttons popping and scattering everywhere on the tiled floor; he put his hand over his heart.

'This tattoo tells everything I think and feel for you, Sally. You are forever my always.'

Sally's eyes stung as she wrapped her arms around his waist and rested her head on his chest. She hugged him tightly then peered up at him with big sorry green eyes, pleading with his confused dark browns to forgive her.

'I love you, baby.' He shook her slightly, as if he was trying to shake sense and his words in to her.

'I know you do, and I love you too. I guess I just thought all this, the house, the proposal, *you* . . . I guess I just thought it was all too good to be true, and I was waiting for the fall back to earth with a bang, and I really thought I got it yesterday when I saw you with her – who, by the way, does have long waist-length hair.' She narrowed her eyes at him. Mal narrowed his eyes right back at her as a silent warning, then took a deep breath and exhaled, clearly exasperated.

'Baby, this', he waved his hands in the air between them, 'is all true. Good, bad, or indifferent, it's all true. So get used to it.' He gripped both her hands, 'We are making up for ten years apart, so we deserve all this and more. And I can't wait for more of you, Sal.' *kiss*

He lifted her off her feet, not breaking the kiss, and with ease carried her to their bedroom. Sally cried and cried again at her stupidity – the insane way she had so quickly distrusted him, Mal, her Mal, who has been nothing but loving, honest, and generous. He was spending his inheritance on a family home for them both and now he had bought her, her very own business, because he loved her so much and wanted to share everything, every bit of his life, love, and happiness with her and only her. How could she have been so speedy to judge him? And out of relief that her worst nightmare wasn't indeed coming to life, she sobbed and sobbed. Mal never stopped kissing her; he just kissed each salty tear that dripped on to her lips, and as each one fell, he kissed her more and more.

'Ring your mum before she has a seizure, Sal. Your dad texted, saying you are to ring her as soon as you're up to it.'

'Ohh, Mal, what will I say?' Sally felt silly and embarrassed.

Mal laughed. 'They know everything, so just say you do too, and everything's sweet now. End off.'

After a long phone call with her mum, she lay back on the bed and rested her head on Mal's chest, her fingers drawing nothing in particular on his tight tummy through his white shirt.

'Why were you so distant the last few weeks, Mal?'

Mal shuffled a little with his legs, then came straight out with it.

'That night in Da Vinci's at our engagement dinner, I thought I saw my dad. A skinnier version, but I recognised him all the same. I had a bloke the solicitor put me in touch with dig about, and yes, it looks like he has come back to Derry, well, Donegal actually.'

'Mal.' The shock in her voice made his name come out as a croak. 'How do you feel about that? Why didn't you just tell me, babes?'

'I didn't know until yesterday if it was really him or not, so I didn't want to add any more on to your plate. You were so excited about the house and that. I didn't want to take anything away from that.'

'But I was so worried about you, thinking all the house business was taking too much out of you. If you would have just told me, babes, then I would not have put you being distant, together with your meeting with Victoria. . . I made a big mess of things.'

Mal frowned and looked down at Sally's waiting eyes. 'I guess am still learning here, babes.' *kiss* . . ."

'Me too.' *kiss*

Chapter 26

'**S**o tell me more about your dad being back.'

They both sat at the coffee table in the living room, their backs to the sofa, bums on the carpet, and legs stretched out under the table, having breakfast of coffee, tea, and croissants. In mid-chew, Mal started telling Sally what he knew.

'He came back from America alone less than a year ago. He's living in Moville in Donegal.'

'So do you think you would want to meet up with him? Get to know him again?'

Mal shuffled slightly. It was a nervous movement she'd only ever seen him do when his father was mentioned.

'I thought of nothing else for the last two weeks, but I don't think I will. I have nothing for him, Sal, no love, no understanding of what he did to my mum and me, nothing. I am just numb to him.'

Sally spoke through the lump in her throat, trying to keep her tone even. She couldn't imagine not having love for her parents or what she would do without them.

'Maybe that's a good thing, Mal. You know that you are so indifferent.'

'Maybe.' *kiss* He pushed the table back with his foot, grasped her two feet, and pulled until she was on her back. 'Now we are behind schedule, my beautiful Sal,' he said, all business like, but Sally knew she was the only business on his mind.

'We are on a schedule?' She giggled and wiggled as he untied the drawstring to her boy-short PJs.

'Yes, I thought we would have had at least five of the rooms christened by now.' kiss kiss kiss

Sunday lunch at Sally's parents' house was cancelled by Mal; he was taking the four of them to Jackson's Hotel for Sunday carvery and to book their wedding, but he didn't mention that bit, although Sally knew by the crafty glint in his dark eyes. Amid was expecting them as they walked through the door, which only confirmed Sally's suspicion. Mal did the introductions, and off they went on a tour of the hotel before lunch. The wedding/function room was stunning; the high ceiling with huge domes held the lighting, which could be changed to match the colour scheme of the wedding party, Amid informed them. The top table area was dressed with fairy lights and chiffon backdrop. Impressive candelabras sat on each round table, and the room had a full-length glass wall that overlooked the hotel gardens, the river Finn, and Drumboe Woods beyond that. Sally went closer to see if she could find the gazebo. When she spotted it further down the garden, she called her mum to look; she couldn't help the grin on her face at the thought of that night.

Mal came up behind Sally, his arms wrapping around her shoulders, caging her in his embrace. 'What you think, Sal? Shall we book it? Amid has an availability for 20th October.'

Sally pivoted in his arms. 'This year?' The shock in her voice was undeniable.

'Oh, Mal, that's not even doable,' said Elizabeth, with even more shock in her voice than Sally had.

'All you two ladies have to do is get dresses. I will do everything else.' kiss

'OK, let's book it.' Sally jumped up into Mal's arms, nestling her head in the crook of his neck and nearly scaring the daylights out of Elizabeth at the same time.

Elizabeth walked into her husband's arms, shaking her head in distress, saying, 'Our baby is getting married in two months' time.' She rested her head on John's chest; then they both took lead from their daughter's excitement.

'If anyone can pull this off, it's Mal,' said John, a note of pride in his voice for his future son-in-law.

'Let's eat,' Mal announced after he put Sally on to her feet again. 'Amid, book the date in your diary, my friend. I am marrying my girl.' Mal's arms were stretched out, as if he was going to break into a song, and everyone laughed at his enthusiasm. Mal handed his credit card over to pay the deposit for the wedding, and Amid offered dinner on him or the hotel, Sally guessed.

'More excitement,' Sally thought; her head was spinning. She hadn't even had a chance to take over the café or finish the décor of the new house, and now this. She found herself looking forward to a normal life, if life would ever be normal with Mal. He was like a bolt of lightning. When he got a thought in his head, he made that thought come to life and very quickly. Not so long ago, her life was depressing her because she never did anything outside of work, gym, Wednesday night girls' night, and the odd wee scatter of girls' nights in or out with Nicole, in which she almost always turned into the third wheel when Johnny got home. Life was boring, and now it was far from it; not that she was complaining, but she couldn't seem to catch a breath between episodes. 'From furniture shopping to wedding dress shopping, here we go,' she thought . . .

Nicole nearly screamed the house down when she heard Sally and Mal had booked their wedding date. She hugged them both, then went back for another hug from Sally. It was Monday evening, and Nicole and Johnny were invited for dinner at Sally and Mal's new home. They brought champagne to toast the house, and it ended in a double celebration.

'How the hell are you going to find a dress in two months, Sally?' asked Nicole when she was settling down to her dinner of salmon, baby potatoes, and roast veg.

'Well, Mum booked an appointment with an up-and-coming wedding dress designer in Dublin. Dad has booked you and your mum and me and mine into a suite at the Shelbourne.'

Nicole squealed again, and Mal nodded to Nicole but asked Johnny, 'Do you not bring earplugs with you to hand out, man?'

Nicole threw him a look, and Johnny dared not laugh.

'Jaysus Mary and Jo, Sally, that's a five-star hotel overlooking St Stephen's Green. I heard they have Egyptian cotton sheets to die for.' Nicole was on a high.

Sally continued, 'I know, Nicole. Mal won't let Dad pay for anything but the dress, so Dad said, "Go and buy what you want and have a great time doing it." So Mum went to town with the credit card already. We drive down Sunday. The appointment is on Monday, and we drive back Tuesday.'

That they did . . .

They had an amazing two nights' stay in the beautiful Shelbourne Hotel and a full day with the dress designer whose name was Kerri – no surname, just Kerri. Kerri had an amazing converted warehouse just off Parnell Square, just walking distance from their hotel, and Sally picked the most amazing dress. White didn't suit her as much as ivory, cream, or champagne did, so white was ruled out quite quickly. Kerri had a great eye for shapes and colours, and nearly everything she recommended was stunning on Sally, but she fell in love with one instantly. It was champagne-coloured silk with off-the-shoulder lace trimming that fell over the top of the dress and stopped at the waist, but at the back, it continued down the full length of the dress in a narrow strip, housing the tiny buttons that ran from the low dip of her back to the end of the slight train. It was stunning and very elegant, and she knew it was 'the one' the minute she stood on the podium and turned to the impressive floor-length antique mirror. Of course, Elizabeth, Nicole, and Anna were tearful and sniffed into their hankies. They finished their champagne and chatted among themselves while a little alterations here and there were done on the dress. After purchasing one elegant wedding dress and one pale pink bridesmaid dress, an amazing hotel stay, and a great laugh had by all, off they went home on a high.

Chapter 27

When Sally got home to Mal, he informed her that her dad had spoken to the priest and booked the same chapel Sally had been attending all her life. Mal had booked two beautiful cars, the silver Rolls Royce Phantom and the classic sliver Bentley R type. He had a band booked, and it just happened that the lead singer's wife made handmade invites, and he had brought some samples home for Sally to look at. He made an appointment to view a photographer's work and had also booked a cameraman to video the whole day and evening. He informed her that Johnny, John, and himself had gone to Different Class menswear and bought suits, but that Nic, Elizabeth, and Sally had to pick the shirts and ties because he didn't know what colour to buy, and the guy in the shop, David, advised them to let the ladies pick them. 'Saves any grief,' David had told them with a wink and a nod that suggested he'd seen it all in his fifty years in the business.

'I am delegating the flowers to your bridesmaid. I draw the line at picking those.'

Sally threw herself on top of him on the sofa where he sat 'You have been busy, babes.' She kissed him. She missed him, and judging from his reaction, he missed her too.

Chapter 28

Mal's business was ready for opening. All the machinery he needed was delivered, and the unit was sectioned off into display areas, work area, and an office space. He did all the work himself, working day and night. Most nights, Sally would bring him dinner from 'The Café' as she had renamed it officially after calling it that the whole time she worked there, instead of having to say Victoria's name in the same sentence (Victoria who *had* cut her hair into a bob). They would eat leftover lasagne and side salad, quiche and baby potatoes, or chilli con carne and rice. She would brush up and dust for him, and they would leave and go home together. One night, lying in Mal's arms in bed, both of them exhausted, she told him she didn't want a honeymoon.

'Why not, babes? Everyone wants a honeymoon, do they not?'

'We are not everyone, and we have hardly had time to breathe the last six months. I want us to stay in Jackson's for two nights, then lock ourselves away in this beautiful home for a few days and just relax with each other.'

Mal blew out a long, relaxing breath and agreed. 'Sounds perfect to me, babes.'

'We have Nicole and Johnny's wedding in the spring, and that's in Greece, so that can double up as our honeymoon. What do you think?' *kiss*

'I take it you're in agreement then?' *kiss*

'Oh yes . . . Having you all to myself whether we are here, in a tent in Culdaff, or the Bahamas, it's all the same to me, Sal.' *kiss*

Mal's next venture was to make the furniture that was to be displayed in the areas he had prepared. That alone took up a lot of his time, time which Sally was envious of, but when she saw the furniture taking shape, she was blown away by his talent and the passion he had for it. He made beds, wardrobes, lockers, chest of drawers, but they all had a unique design or shape, and Mal made it look effortless. He had a catalogue of furniture he had made in Spain on his computer, which he would use to show potential customers, but he needed to display his work also, and it was starting to take shape. He was advertising for Christmas orders but wasn't actually opening the shop up until after the wedding. He called into the training centre, where he had started his training after leaving school. He got chatting with his old lecturer and asked him to recommend a young fella to take on as his apprentice. A tall skinny boy called Sean was top on the list. Christmas came early for Sean because Mal hired him on the spot, but on the condition that he continued his day release at the training centre too to finish his course.

Nicole took her bridesmaid duties very seriously and took over the flowers for the wedding. Sally left her to it. She knew colours and the outfits, so there was no one more qualified than her to bring it all together. The rings were being made. The songs were picked for the chapel and first dance (Westlife had to get in there somewhere). Nicole's girls from the salon were coming to do hair and make-up for the bride, bridesmaid, and mums. The guest list went on and on from Sally's side, but Mal was the only name on his side. Mal said it didn't bother him in the slightest and that Johnny was going to be his best man and that he was the closest thing to a best friend he had ever had apart from Sally.

Sally took off early from 'The Café' and went straight to Mal's unit, soon-to-be shop, with dinner; she sat in the office chair, and he chose to sit on the deck next to her, eating a jacket potato with chilli beef and salad out of the yellow polystyrene takeaway container. They were flicking through his new web site when a soft rattle came at the door before it opened. A man in his early sixties stood in the door frame. Tension and silence filled the room as the two men eyeballed each other, the older man's face a lot less taut than the younger's. Right then, Sally could see that Mal wasn't as indifferent as he thought he was. She knew exactly who the man was. Sally stood to break the silence and extended her hand.

'Hello, Mr Quinn, I am Sally, Mal's fiancée.' Sally had never met the man before. She had only ever been introduced to Mal's mother when they were dating.

'Thank you,' he replied, taking her hand, 'you're a lovely young lady.'

Mal managed to move his lips after a while, and venting his anger he spoke, 'What do you want, old man?'

'Mal!' Sally was shocked at his reaction; it was so disrespectful. The man smiled shyly at Sally.

'I couldn't believe it when I heard your name on the radio in the advertisements for this place. I knew it had to be you. You were always so talented.'

'Ha, save the praise. You're about ten years too late.' Mal turned his back on them both, looking out the office window at the display area.

'I am sorry, Son.'

'Don't you son me. You gave up that right long ago.' Mal's body never moved a muscle as he spoke. He stood poker straight, the neat window frame of his office dwarfed by his own huge bulk of a frame.

'Please just give me a chance to talk, to explain to you. I . . . I know I will never have a good enough reason for leaving you like I did. I was selfish, but I would like to build a bridge now, if you would only let me.'

Mal stayed silent, looking out the window, still as a statue. When the silence had said enough, Mal's dad reached into the pocket of his overcoat and handed Sally a piece of paper with his name, address, and phone number on it. Sally took it, and thinking quick on her feet, she handed Martin a business card back, nodding to it, silently saying, 'Call him.' Just before Martin left, Sally watched his eyes focus on her necklace, the one Mal had given her in Culdaff, which belonged to his mum. She saw the recognition in his eyes, but he didn't comment. Martin left the office and building.

Mal turned to Sally. 'You ready to go?'

Sally tidied up their leftover dinner, and he lifted his keys and locked up, not a word spoken. They had both cars with them, so Sally had to wait to get home to talk to him. When they got home, she ran a bath, and they both got in, still in a hush of silence, but they both knew that was about to end.

Mal spoke first. 'What are you thinking, Sally? I can hear your brain ticking in overdrive.' He had only a small smile for her.

'Am thinking it's been ten years, and maybe it's time to have a chat with him and that it's a sign that you both returned to Derry–Donegal in the same year more or less.' Sally watched her words sink in. 'What are you thinking, Mal? That's what is most important here.'

'Am thinking I want to bury myself in you right here in this bath.'

'Mal!' She swatted him, bubbles floating in the air. 'Be serious and stop evading the topic. It's important.'

'Yeah, I might call him.' He shocked her into silence again. 'With the wedding and that coming up, I think it would be kinda nice if things worked out and he could come.'

'Jesus, you never fail to surprise me.' Sally shook her head in disbelief at the 180-degree turnaround in such a short time; she had expected she would have to talk him into meeting with Martin and that it would take weeks, maybe months. He grabbed her wrists and with a swoosh of the water and bubbles she was on his lap, sitting astride him.

'I promise to never stop surprising you, baby.' *kiss*

Next morning in his office, the phone was ringing by the time he got to it; it rang off but rang straight away again. Martin didn't give Mal long to get his head around things. (So that's where Mal got his fireball personality from.)

'Hello, Son' was the opening line.

'Too early for son, but let's meet up.' Martin's laughter filled Mal's ears and strangely filled his heart too. 'Come to the house tonight for dinner.' Mal gave him the address and agreed seven would suit both parties. He came off the phone with a light-hearted feeling that he kinda liked. He texted Sally.

Martins coming for dinner at 7 x

What? Seriously? Jeez surprised AGAIN. Great babes delighted for u xx

Lol, I promised didn't I x

That you did. Can't wait. What sud I cook? Xx

We will cook sumthin together I will go to sainsburys after work. C u at home bout 5.30 x

Chapter 29

Martin was there on the dot to seven, armed with chocolates, flowers, and wine. Sally kissed him on the cheek and thanked him for the gifts. Mal shook his hand at the door and welcomed him in.

'Great house you kids have here.' Martin was impressed, looking around as they walked through to the kitchen.

When they sat at the table (which Mal had fixed, but they had to order new chairs), the small chat was a bit much for Mal, so he piped up, asking, 'What happened with America then?'

Martin's light nature faded and his nostrils flared. Mal was like his mum in looks, but he most definitely had his dad's personality and mannerisms. Sally could tell just looking at Martin that he was just as big of a fireball as his son was.

'Let's just say the *lady* I went out there to got what she wanted and left me.' The anger in his voice and the way he spat the word *lady* told Sally it was still a sore subject.

Mal laughed a sarcastic forced laugh; Sally nearly flipped at Mal's disrespect for his own father.

'Hell, rub it up, ye!' Mal lifted his beer in a toast, and Martin returned the gesture with his glass of wine, also laughing.

'I deserve that I suppose.'

Sally relaxed; the ice was broken and the conversation was easy. They sat down to a meal of lasagne, salad, and wedges; the smell was filling the kitchen and making their mouths water. They finished up their meal and Sally was chatting to Martin about The Café as she dished out dessert – homemade orange and dark chocolate ice cream and carrot cake.

'We are getting married 20ᵗʰ October. If you are free, you are welcome to come.' Mal shrugged in a carefree movement and took a swig of beer.

For a few seconds, Martin was stunned, and Sally thought she saw a tear or two glaze his eyes a little. Then he cleared his throat. 'Of course, I would love to be there, thank you. It means a lot, thank you.' He nodded to Sally. Then nodding again to her necklace, he said, 'That's your mother's?'

Without waiting for an answer, he spoke again, 'I bought that for her the day you were born.'

Mal and Martin both stared at Sally, both not wanting to look at the other man's expression.

'She loved it, never left it off her.'

Silence fell over the room. Sally felt all eyes on her and on her neck. She felt uncomfortable and broke the silence by saying, 'I love it too. It's so precious and even more so now that we know the story behind it.' She walked to Mal and put her hand on his shoulder and rubbed it, hoping she was comforting him. 'Don't you think?' She looked up at Mal.

Mal opened another beer and changed the subject . . .

Dinner went well considering that two days before Mal was determined not to see his dad.

'Come for dinner again, Martin, before the wedding, and I will invite my mum and dad too.'

Sally was buzzing that Mal would have his dad at the wedding. One person didn't make up for the rest of the 100 guests being from her side, but it would be nice for Mal to have his dad there on his wedding day.

Chapter 30

September had flown by. It gave way to October without any warning whatsoever. 1ˢᵗ October freaked Sally out. That morning started with the alarm being switched off instead of being put on snooze; she got mascara on her fingers and rubbed it all over her nose and had to redo her make-up. The coffee from the machine, which was timed for her leaving the house so she could function on her way to work, was now cold, and she could only find one work shoe. She was cursing at every turn, and as Mal walked towards her with a fresh coffee in one hand and her missing shoe in the other, she burst into tears. Mal put both down and wrapped her up in his arms.

'Hey . . . hey . . . what's up, baby?'

It took her a few beats before she found her tongue. 'It's just beginning to get too much. I mean, the wedding, the café, the house, am grateful for them all, but it's a lot to take on in a very short space of time,' she blurted out in a rush. 'Am sorry, Mal, I sound ungrateful, but am really not.'

'Shh, you don't, baby. It is a lot to take on, but it will be all worth it. I promise. OK?' He dipped to look into her eyes.

'Yes, of course, it will, am just having a bad morning.' Off she went to work, trying hard to shake the stress.

Then entered Michael . . .

'Hey, good looking, you still seeing that big ape?'

Lisa, Sally's colleague and now employee, laughed, saying, 'She's marrying him for God's sake, the lucky bitch.'

Sally just rolled her eyes at Lisa's reference to her love life and smiled at Michael.

'Yes and yes, I am marrying him in a few weeks' time.'

Michael couldn't hide the shock on his face or his voice.

'Ohh, you up the duff or something, what's the hurry?'

'No!' said Sally, horrified, and she stormed off into the office.

On a normal day, she could deal with Michael, she had been for the last two years, but today, she just couldn't shake herself. His words were haunting her even after lunch and into the evening. 'Was everyone going to think that? Was everyone going to think I got myself pregnant and that's why I was marrying Mal so soon?' These questions were spinning around in her head when Mal came home that evening.

'Hey, babes, why did you not call to the shop after work?'

'Am just tired. Sorry.'

'Hey.' He lifted her off the sofa where she was curled up and walked upstairs, put her on the vanity surround at the sink, and started to run the bath. 'You still stressed out from this morning?'

Sally shook her head, unwelcome and uncalled for tears springing to her eyes again and making her feel silly and weak, but she couldn't help them. 'Everyone's going to think I am pregnant, and that's why we are marrying so quickly,' she blurted out.

'Who gives a shit what people think, Sal?' He was standing right in front of her, brushing her tears away. 'If you were, would you be disappointed?'

'What? No . . . I . . . I mean, I never thought about it. I don't know. You?' Sally's voice was on high volume and high speed.

'Sally, I told you I can't wait for more of you, and if that means more in the form of a baby, then I'll be the most ecstatic man alive. Don't cry, babes. You'll make me sad.' He pouted, looking down into her face and kissing her with swift little kisses.

Sally's heart lightened, and she giggled at his pout. 'You soo do not suit pouting.'

'I know, am too manly, right?' he laughed and felt a small accomplishment at getting her to laugh too. They bathed together, went downstairs, made cheese toasties for handiness, and went straight to bed, exhausted again but in better form.

Sally's stress level was up and down like a yoyo over the weeks to come; she was short with everyone and blamed the wedding and workload that both Mal and she had on. She was interviewing for a new café assistant, and no one was up to her standards. She couldn't take time off for the wedding until she found someone. Chloe, the girl renting her apartment, text her, asking about the job, and Sally instantly got a good feeling about the idea. Chloe was clean and tidy, chatty, and fun. She promised she was a hard worker, and since she already had a background in catering and waitressing, she sounded perfect. Sally went with her gut feeling and hired her on a three-month trial.

On Wednesday morning, one week and three days to go to the big day, Elizabeth text Sally, Nicole, and Anna.

Pampering nite tonite in my house xx

Sally threw a quick text back.

K. time?

You're welcome . . . 7

Sorry xx ok c u then xx

Nicole already knew, as it was her girls from the salon coming out to do the pampering. Nicole had ordered bathrobes with their names and ranks in the wedding on the backs. Elizabeth's, of course, read 'mother of the bride', Nicole's was 'bridesmaid', Anna's was 'mother of the bridesmaid', and Sally's read 'the bride'. They had champagne and wine chilling; chocolates, nuts, cheese, and crackers displayed; and bathrobes on when Sally came through the door. She was surprised and delighted to see the effort they all had gone to; she loved the bathrobes and wasted no time in getting into hers. The girls had also bought a plastic dress-up tiara with a cheap net veil and put it on Sally's head, just for fun and photos. Nicole's girls started to work their magic. They did facials, massages, and nails. The girls laughed and drank champagne for a toast and then had wine and nibbles before taking lots of selfies, deleting most of them because they had either no make-up on or a face mask was crumbling, which wasn't a good look on anyone.

Sally's dad came home; he had stayed as long as he could in his office. Sally jumped up to hug her dad as he came through the door.

'Daa-dee, am getting married next week. Can ye beeve it?' She was slurring her words and hanging off John's neck.

John made eyes at Elizabeth, but knew as he looked at the rest of them that they didn't have too much to drink. Just at that, Sally was sick everywhere – all over John's expensive suit trousers and shoes, the hall carpet, up the walls, everywhere.

'Sorry da-dee,' she slurred again.

John scooped her in his arms and carried her to the bathroom. Elizabeth took over by washing her face and neck while John went to get a quick change.

'I hardly ate all day,' Sally whispered as John then carried her to her old room and laid her in her bed. Elizabeth put a bin beside her bed and tucked her little girl in, probably for the last time in her old bed as Sally Mc Quire.

John phoned Mal, and just as John expected, Mal came straight over and climbed into bed beside Sally, ready to be on call if needed. Next morning, Sally woke with a thumping headache and a belly like a washing machine on full spin.

'I didn't think I drank that much.' Her voice was weak.

'I know, baby.' Mal and Elizabeth had already had this conversation before Elizabeth popped to the shops that morning. Mal just stroked her forehead and offered sips of water now and again. When Mal heard Elizabeth's car pull into the drive, he went down to meet her coming through the door.

'You got it?'

'Yes, want me to come with you?' Elizabeth's eyes were full of concern.

'Naw, I got this. Thanks, Elizabeth.'

Sally was sitting up in bed when Mal got back.

'Sal, I think you better take this.' He pulled a pregnancy test from a paper bag and offered it to her . . .

Chapter 31

Two minutes later, they were sitting on the edge of the bed, holding hands and staring at the wee white stick that could change their lives forever. Mal had turned it to face down until the three minutes were up. 'Two blue lines mean pregnant, one blue line, not pregnant. Ready?'

She nodded back at him, unable to put two words together. He flipped it over.

'Yes, baby, yes,' Mal was shouting and punching the air before he looked at Sally for her reaction. He dropped to his knees in front of her, his hands on her hands resting on her lap. 'You OK, Sal? Baby, you OK?'

She was in a state of shock; the only thing she could get out of her mouth was the water she was sipping at all morning, and it landed right on Mal's lap.

'Shit, baby.' He was half laughing, half shocked as the liquid soaked through him; he stripped out of his jeans in two seconds flat and had her in his arms again, calling Elizabeth at the top of his voice. Elizabeth came bursting through the door of the bedroom, with the question written all over her face that she had been waiting all morning to be answered.

'You're going to be a granny, Elizabeth,' Mal announced, not able to contain his excitement one bit. Sally still hadn't spoken. Elizabeth dropped to her knees in front of her.

'Oh, darling, that's great news. Are you OK, darling?'

'Am in shock, Mum.'

'I know, darling, but it's a good shock, yes?'

'I guess so. I mean, am not prepared for this. I don't know what to feel.'

Mal hugged Sally and Elizabeth tighter than he actually intended. 'Baby, this is going to be brilliant. Aww, I love you so much, and you are going to be a great mum.' Mal's excitement was too big for the room; it was through the roof.

Elizabeth hugged her daughter too and whispered in her ear, 'Everything's going to be just fine, darling.' She told Sally to go for a shower, and she started to change the bed and clean up the liquid evidence of her daughter's shock. Mal was still running around in his boxer shorts but didn't seem to notice; he was on the phone with John when Elizabeth handed him a pair of John's sweatpants and nodded to them, silently telling him to *get dressed*.

When Sally had her shower, she felt a lot better. She had breakfast of coffee and croissants and seemed to keep them down. They drove home, Mal buzzing in the seat beside her. She allowed herself to get a little excited too, now that the sickness had left her. She couldn't help but buzz off Mal buzzing.

'A wee baby, Mal, I can't believe it.'

'I know, baby, it's all my dreams and more coming true.'

'Oh my God, my dress, what if it doesn't fit?'

'Baby, the wedding is next week, and you never did put the weight back on that you lost when I was in hospital. You will be fine, better than fine, *hot, hot, hot.*' He patted her leg, parked the car in the drive, and ran round and opened the car door for her; then he led her to the front door of their home.

'This is a great house to bring up children.' Mal hugged Sally at the front door. 'I love you so much, baby. I can't tell you enough, but I promise I will die trying to convince you just how much.' *kiss*

Sally phoned in to work and told them she was taking the day off, and Mal did the same. He phoned Sean and told him to man the phones and clean up, then take the rest of the day off too. They sat on their big cosy sofa and watched reruns of *Husbands of Hollywood* and *Friends*, laughing and giggling and kissing all day long.

'No more booze for you then, baby,' Mal piped up.

'I know,' Sally huffed, 'but it will be worth it.'

She rubbed at her tummy, and Mal got between her legs, his head at her belly, and whispered, 'I love you already, little one.'

Sally's heart swelled and tears pricked her eyes; tears of joy and contentment filled her, and she rubbed and tugged at Mal's overlong hair.

'Go get a haircut, you fur ball,' she teased him.

He crawled up her body and took her mouth with the softest of lips, calm and gentle, worshipping her with every lick and dip of his tongue – thanking her silently for all she had already given him, for the happiness, the contentment, her love, and now for the baby she was going to bring into the world, his baby, whom he would love and cherish and never ever leave behind. They would both share his name, his life, and his dreams, and he would in return share theirs, because nothing or nobody was going to take his wife and baby away from him. Nothing would stop him from loving them like he loved them in this very minute. For the rest of his life, he would dedicate his every breath to them both.

Now and forever . . .

2 Years and 8 months later. . .

'*I have to keep* telling myself this isn't a dream,' Mal said to Sally, and not for the first time in the last few years.

He had said it on the day of their wedding when Sally's dad, John, walked her up the aisle and handed her hand over into his. He looked Sally up and down in awe, leant in, and whispered it in her ear.

He said it the morning after the wedding and that night again as they got into the huge big bed in the honeymoon suite they had booked for three nights, complete with chocolate fountain.

On the way back from the midwife appointment that booked Sally into the midwife's books at ten weeks pregnant, he blew out a puff of air and said it again then.

When Sally started to get a small bump, he was lying on top of the bed, rubbing her tummy and singing 'Twinkle, twinkle little star', and he whispered it to her belly then.

There were loads of times, and Sally got to predict the statement from him in different situations before he even said it. The biggest shock was when they went for their twenty-three-week scan and the doctor said, 'Oh, we have two heartbeats.'

'Oh, we have what?' croaked Sally.

'What?' spat Mal.

'Two heartbeats. Congratulations, Mr and Mrs Quinn, you're having twins.'

He said it to John and Elizabeth that day over and over again.

Now planning and preparing for the twins' second birthday party, he walked into the kitchen where Sally was making Mars Bar cakes and snaked his arms around Sally's waist, and he nibbled on her neck and shoulders and said it again.

'I know,' said Sally, arching her neck back for more kisses. 'It's hard to believe they are two already.' *kiss*

'Where are they?' *kiss*

'Out on the bouncy castle with your dad.' *kiss*

'Could we sneak upstairs?' *kiss*

'No.' *kiss*

'Spoilsport.' *kiss*

'You have no shame.' *kiss*

Sally turned in his arms, giggling. 'I love you, babes.'

'If you love me, you will come upstairs with me, righ—'

He didn't get to finish the sentence as Elizabeth and John came through the front door, John calling to Mal to help him with the presents.

'Maybe later, babes,' she giggled with a promise in the statement.

And she laughed again as he sulked and walked towards the front door, his shoulders slumped. The next thing Sally saw were two motorised Ride on BMW lookalike jeeps, with two 'happy second birthday' balloons tied to them, taking up the kitchen floor. The twins came running in, Cormac shouting, 'Mum', and Conan shouting, 'Dad.' They were about to tell on each other when they spied the jeeps and ran towards them instead.

'Look, Mum. Look, Dad.' The excitement was pounding through their wee bodies.

'What do you two say to Nanna and Pops?'

'Tank you', 'tank you' went the wee voices of the two cutest, adorable, crazy wee boys in the world. Their dad, Pops (John), and Gan-ga (Martin) took the jeeps to the side of the house and let them race up and down the length of the drive. Cormac wore a Spiderman top, and Conan wore a Batman top, both with capes at the back, which made the boys, in their jeeps on the driveway, look like they were on the set of a children's action movie. The boys were buzzing. Elizabeth went about setting the adults' table of nibbles and drinks, and Sally set the kids' table with sweets, crisps, chocolates, and jugs of juice. She set the cake in the middle of the table. It was a three-tier – Spiderman, Batman, Cormac and Conan – cake. Batman was down one side and Spiderman down the other and on the top was a photo scanned on the icing of Cormac's face painted like Spiderman and of Conan's face painted like Batman, both faces squashed together spreading the paint; it was so cute and the perfect picture for the top of the cake.

'Nic and Johnny are here,' Mal called in through the conservatory to the kitchen.

Nicole made it to the kitchen, past the boys and their toys, with Lily-Ann on her hip. She was nine months old and cute as a button. She had the biggest pink bow hairband on her wee bald but auburn head and a pink dress with knickers to match. Nicole and Johnny were the twins' godparents, and Sally and Mal were Lily-Ann's, just as Sally and Nicole had promised each other from the time when they were of no age.

Nicole's wedding in Greece was just as anyone could have imagined – 'a fairy tale'. It took place on the beach; she wore a white gipsy-style off-the-shoulder white wedding dress and Johnny reluctantly wore a light beige trousers and waistcoat duo and white shirt. (Nicole gave in to him not wearing a tie eventually.) She had baby's breath (everlasting love) weaved through her auburn hair, which would have looked pure 80s, but Nicole pulled it off. Nicole planned her wedding for the start of March so Sally could still fly and still be her bridesmaid. Sally wore a short lemon maternity bridesmaid dress and felt very comfortable, cool, and girlie in it.

On 11 June, the twins were born, and life as they knew it was a lot different. Today, looking back, Sally didn't know how she had got through that year – from the minute Mal stood outside her mum and dad's mobile home in Culdaff to the day the twins were born, never mind after that. It was fast, crazy, and non-stop drama and head rushes, but she thought that every head rush and drama was worth everything she has right here today.

The twins, Lily-Ann, and a few of their wee play friends from the crèche they go to three days a week when Sally works had a great time on the bouncy castle and the jeeps; they wrecked everything they laid their eyes and chocolate-stained hands on in the playroom and most of the house. The sweets and chocolate really did kick in tenfold. Sally was exhausted by the time everyone left, and it was just Mal and her with a twin each sleeping on their laps. Mal took them one by one up to their custom-made beds. Mal made them a bed each in the shape of a train. Each bed was in total length ten feet long because of the driving cabs at the front of the actual beds with their names carved along the top. He also had made their bedroom furniture to match, with trains carved out in the wood, instead of handles for the drawers and the wardrobe door. The room was a work of art, and the boys loved it all.

When Mal got back to the living area, Sally had fallen asleep too, so he scooped her up in his arms and carried her up to bed too. He lay on top of the bed, looking at her sleep. He thought back to the first time she had said she loved him, in the field of Lenamore stables, to the first day he saw her again after the ten years he was deprived of her, to now. They were meant to be together; all that time apart, he had always known it. He felt her every day. He felt her breathing and living; thousands of miles away, he knew she wouldn't ever belong to anyone else but him. He willed her heart every day to hold out for him. His heart did and always would belong to her, and she belonged in it with his boys locked up in his heart and soul, just the four of them. Sally stirred a little, and Mal kissed her awake.

'Oh, am so tired, babes. I fell asleep on you.'

'It's OK, baby. I was just enjoying looking and admiring you as you slept.' *kiss*

'What were you thinking about?' Sally knew he had a look in his eyes.

'I was thinking how beautiful you are and how lucky I am to have you.' kiss 'And the twins.' *kiss* 'And how I love us.' *kiss* 'And how perfect we are.' *kiss* 'The four of us are just perfect.' *kiss*

Sally sat up on the bed, looking puzzled. 'Really?'

Now Mal looked puzzled too. 'Yeah, perfect. Why?'

'Ohh, I don't know. There's something missing.'

'What? What's missing?' Mal looked worried now, and Sally couldn't help but tease a little more.

'Well, I was thinking that there's just something. I just can't put my finger on it. Do you not feel it too?'

'Bloody hell, Sal, no, I can't feel it. What's up, babes? I think it just can't get any more perfect than right now.'

Sally moved slightly to reach into the drawer of her nightstand, and with a cheeky grin, she purred, 'More perfect.' And with pride written all over her face, she produced a white stick with two blue lines.

Mal nearly fell off the bed as he jumped to punch the air and then fell back on to the bed and rolled Sally under him.

'You . . .' *kiss* 'Are . . .' *kiss* 'The . . .' *kiss* 'Most . . .' *kiss* 'Perfect . . .' kiss 'Of all.' *kisses* . . ."

The End

'Those Blues'

CHAPTER ONE

*F*iona Michaels sits in the front row of St Patrick's Cathedral, Dublin in silent torment, listening…

Her secret and silent, invisible revenge on her husband was that she had the reddest, sexiest, boldest underwear on under her LBD.

His friends and family and even her family don't have a clue. They all think she is beside herself with grief… If they only knew!

"Dave lived his life for his wife Fiona and his business. He was a hard worker and loved the business he was in but even more than his business, he loved Fiona. From the moment he met her he was besotted, so his best friend and work colleague tells me." Father Mc Cay delivered his eulogy in a sincere, genuine voice, not sounding at all like he does this nearly every day of his priesthood life. He then looks in Fiona's direction with a sympathetic nod. She nods attentively back at him, with a silent inward snarl. Not at father Mc Cay but at the thought of who and what was in the heavy pine box in full view of the one hundred plus family and some vultures that have come to pay their last respects, (her to make sure the bastard is really dead) to her husband.

Fiona's heart was numb. Her head pounded with the pressure of keeping up appearances and her mind was in over drive with thoughts of her dancing on his grave with nothing on but her reddest, sexiest, boldest underwear. 'Father Mc Cay' she thought 'If you only knew you were burying the devil himself this day.'

Dave Michaels was a horrid man and came from a long line of them seemingly. Dave and his father before him both worked hard and both had the gift of the gap and an even bigger gift of making money, they made friends and money like they were going out of style, as they say.

Dave's father, Zac Michaels was a stockbroker in the early '90's' in London's Canary Wharf. He had 'the lot,' a beautiful wife, two beautiful sons and a glorious reconstructed townhouse in central London that any super star would be proud to call home. When his client's came to town with their wife's Zac would throw a dinner party at his home, show off his own wife and his palatial townhouse. But, with the drugs and whore's was where the real deals were clinched and the big money made.

Dave Michaels followed in his dad's footsteps in many ways. He studied finance and got a job as a finance adviser. Having his contacts in the investment world he roared to the top of his game and soon made enough money to set up his own firm. On a stag weekend to Dublin his stone heart got captured by his very own 'Molly Malone.' After his father died a cruel early death at the hands of throat cancer he up and moved to Dublin to set up his firm, financial advising the people of Dublin. Not before looking for Fiona. He wined, dined and talked the talk and eventually got Fiona up the aisle within six months.

Jane Michaels, Dave's mum died when the boys were only young, in a house fire. She had taken the boys to a friend's house in Cordon to get away from her husband's drug infested rampage at their beautiful home. The boys were put to bed in the guest room on the ground floor and Jane and her friend, Jill sat in the living area on the top floor chatting, poor Jane poured her heart out for the first time ever about her husband and his demons. Jill sat listening with a patient ear and smoked her brains out at the same time. The last cig did the lethal damage.

The two boys then ten and twelve, were rescued by a brave neighbour but Jane and Jill never made it out alive.

At twelve years old Dave looked out for his younger brother and allow they had happy memories of their mum, his dad soon tarnished them, filling the boy's heads with twisted evil stories of her, adding that she took the boys to that house that night because she was going to run away with another man. The man was going to fly the boys to Mexico and sell them as slaves. The boy's believed every word from their father as he had the gift of manipulating people and situations to his own advantage.

Fiona went from being an easy going, light hearted, business women of twenty-nine, to a hard hearted emotionless zombie albeit a very good looking and well-presented zombie. With a 5"10 slim frame, a long, swan neck line and now short cropped locks which she fixed behind her ears to show off one of her most stunning assets, her eyes, some people would say she was Emma Willis's spit. Her eyes were a light blue sometimes like a light grey. Anyone that looked Fiona Michaels in the eye was captured at once. Be it with admiration, fascination or envy, some men lusted on the spot.

After modelling for nine years through university and after, she got sick of it but not the business so she seen an opening, four years previously and used her own savings to start small and build her own model agency, 'Model First'. Now a very well respected business. Her degree in business at Trinity College paid off, she was smart and beautiful and people admired that, her models were well looked after and she was on a friendly basis with them all to a certain degree, just enough to have the respect she deserved as a boss. A few girls that got on their high and mighty horses were soon brought down to earth respectfully. Fiona's right hand lady was Tara and Tara's right hand man was Co-co as in Cornelius but that was much too masculine for him so he shortened it to Co-co as in Chanel not the clown.

Tara and Fiona worked a great team of both men and women. Their work ethnic was quite similar but it also differed from time to time which work out well, they would call on Co-co if a decision was not getting resolved. He would inflict drama into the situation and with a very flamboyant air of importance he always delivered the goods or a good reason for a certain decision at least.

Lightning Source UK Ltd.
Milton Keynes UK
UKOW04f1254110216

268163UK00001B/45/P